T0244766

1

Kingsley R. Johnson
kingsleyjohnnson.author@gmail.com

DEADLY GREENS

by

Kingsley R. Johnson

60,195 Words

DEADLY GREENS

BY

KINGSLEY R. JOHNSON

I would like to express my sincere gratitude to my family for their support.

TABLE OF CONTENTS

CHAPTER ONE

THE PERFECT DAY

It was one of those special days on the golf course. The sky was a brilliant blue without a cloud to be seen. Along with the freshly mowed green grass, the canvas was complete. Everything was working for me today. My drives were straight down the middle of the fairway. I was reading the greens so perfectly that my putts looked like there was a groove in the green to the hole. It was the type of day that you were happy to be alive.

I made a side bet with Jake and Ray for a nice cool creamy Guinness which they already owed me for a birdie putt I made back on the Par-4 Sixteenth. I reached down to repair the divot from where my ball landed. I was about 115 yards out which was perfect for my pitching wedge. I had enough backspin on the ball to get me right into position. All I had to do was sink this four-foot birdie putt on this Par-5 signature hole and the boys would have to pay up.

Just before I was ready to putt, Jake yelled, "Hey Clancy, you want to go double or nothing?"

"Sure, I'll take your money," I said.

I wasn't worried about the putt at all. Especially since I was making my putts all day long. It was the murders that kept me from concentrating on this putt. As soon as I hit the ball, I knew I missed it. I pulled it to the left and it lipped out.

"Pay up Clancy!" Ray shouted.

"Not a problem guys." It's the only hole you two won." I said.

"We saved the best for last," Jake said.

This was our normal outing with the Pinewood Golf Association. Normally we have about twenty guys who show up every weekend to play. It's great, all you do is call the 'hotline' to find out what course we're playing, leave your name and just show up. I've been a member for over ten years.

Pinewood was formed back in the late sixties. Mike Gibson was the founding member and president of Pinewood. It was established so that Blacks could get a chance to play golf. Back in the day, it was hard for us to get on a golf course unless we were caddies or worked in the kitchen. The racism was so rampant back then. The only way around it was this loophole that Mike found. It was illegal to discriminate against associations. When Black people tried to get tee times on their own or just show up at the golf course, they were not allowed to play. However, Mike found a way. Mike was one of the first Black attorneys in Spokane, Washington. He found a bylaw that all city and public golf courses had to abide by. 'It stated that all clubs, organizations, and associations that are legally established with a charter of laws and regulations for the use of all public facilities and are filed with the state and county are entitled to all the benefits and use of all public facilities.' Amazingly, these four Black men grew Pinewood to over 250 members today. And, that word would spread to other states as well. Different chapters of Black golf associations were formed all over the entire West Coast and eventually the whole country and even Canada.

Since there was such a small minority population in Spokane, the group would get all sorts of stares and jeers from all the white players.

That was then, and this is now. The Diamondback Golf and Country Club is a new course; only five years old. The course is in great shape because they are getting ready to host the U.S. Senior Open to be held here in three weeks.

I looked over at Jake and said, "You may have won a couple of beers from me, but this is the easiest money I made today." Jake wasn't too happy because he knew that I was going to make about $70.00 in skins; that is bets. We always gamble when we're out here playing. It wouldn't be golf if we didn't have a friendly wager or two. There is a pot that everyone chips in, and we usually have side bets as well, like the two beers I owe Jake. I know Jake was happy that he would get something today besides being frustrated by the terrible day he had.

"Clancy, all I want to know, are you going to give me a chance to win some of my money back?" Jake asked.

"You know I will."

"You're too kind Clancy."

I was glad that we were finally at the 18th green. I've been a member at Diamondback for the last two years thanks to Al Jackson. Al picked up the $20,000.00 membership dues for the first two years. After that, I am responsible for making the payment. It's a beautiful place to play. Besides, Al owes me since I saved his life when we were serving together with the Marines in Iraq during the first Gulf War.

My friend, Al 'Long Ball' Jackson hired me. My name is Harry Clancy, I'm a private investigator here in Spokane. Al's been playing on the Senior Tour for the past four years. His first three years were great. Al just turned fifty-four and won two of the major tournaments his first year out. The next year was even better. He won three majors. He was on fire. However, this year he's been in a slump. Al hasn't broken into the top ten. He says his game is off because of the threats.

He believes someone is out to kill him. Over the past six months three people have been killed: all black. One on the men's PGA Tour, a woman on the LPGA Tour, and a member of the Oregon State men's golf team. To say the least, Al's a little nervous is an understatement.

I looked at my scorecard, 74, not bad, I said to myself. I owe a lot to Long Ball. If it wasn't for him and all the help he gave me with my game, I wouldn't be here. Plus, the fact I saved him from having an Iraqi soldier shoot him when his weapon jammed might make him feel a little bit obligated.

"You better show up next week Clancy! I want a chance to win some of my money back," Jake said.

"Maybe, maybe not, who's to say," I said with a smirk on my face. I know that upsets Jake; he hates to lose. But I do love to take their money now. For many years, these guys used to take my money. I remember one year when we had our annual club championship I came in last place. I got the 'Golden Toilet Award.' Not only was I embarrassed, but both Jake and Ray had their fair share of laughs at my expense. Because of that experience Long Ball and I got close. Long Ball worked with me on my short game, my drives, and most importantly, my putting. He was a great coach. If it wasn't for him, they would still be taking my money.

We all shook hands after Ray made the last putt.

"That was fun guys. Let's go inside and cool off with some beers. I guess I'm buying you a couple of beers Jake," I said with a smile on my face.

As we were walking onto the cart path off the eighteenth green you could hear the starter announcing the foursome to tee off, "Morgan, next on the tee. Followed by the Taylor twosome and the Riley twosome on deck."

You could hear the whack of the golf balls being hit as we walked by the driving range. Several golfers on the practice green were taking their last putts before being told that it was their turn to tee off.

As I was opening the door to the clubhouse, I could feel the rush of cool air from the air conditioner inside when my cell phone rang. I could tell by the caller ID that it was Long Ball.

"Hey Long Ball, how are you doing my friend?" I asked as I was walking inside.

"How much money did you win today, Clancy?" he asked.

"I took Jake and Ray for about $70.00."

"Good job," he said. "You're doing what I told you to do, aren't you?"

"You know it. I can't tell you how much your pointers have helped me to knock strokes off my game. I shot a 74 today."

"Fantastic Clancy, that's great."

I've always considered Long Ball as my mentor. And it feels good to hear your teacher give you praise when you do something right.

"I wish you could have seen me today LB. I was in the zone. I knew when I addressed the ball, I was going to hit it dead solid perfect."

"Don't worry Clancy, I'll be there next week, and I'll get a chance to see you hit. I'm going to drive up. I need to take it easy for a few days before the Open."

"What's the matter?" I can always tell when something is wrong with Long Ball.

"You haven't changed a bit Clancy. You can read me like a book."

"You know that's right."

"Hold on Long Ball, I was just about to go inside the clubhouse when you called. I'm going back outside so we can have some privacy," I didn't want everyone to overhear our conversation. I can tell he is upset.

"I'm going to drive up after the funeral."

"What funeral? Is it your mother?" I asked.

"No, not her, she's fine. It's my niece."

"Not Nina?"

"Clancy, haven't you been watching the news?"

"You mean about the coed getting killed at Stanford?"

"Yes."

"What about it?"

"Here name was Nina Jackson, my niece. She was murdered last night."

"Long Ball, I am so sorry. I saw on the TV this morning that someone was killed, but I didn't stick around to listen to the rest of the story. We had a 7:20 tee time and I was running late. I flicked off the TV."

Nina was the second highest-ranked collegiate athlete in women's golf. She was Long Ball's protégé. He worked with her since she was twelve years old. He taught her everything he knew. Nina was a natural. She won the state championship in high school and eventually got a scholarship to play at Stanford.

"Clancy, she is the fourth Black golfer murdered in the last six months. The other golfers were Joey Conrad from Oregon State, Kris Montgomery, from the LPGA and Charles 'The Panther' Mackey on the PGA. It's got me worried. If this guy continues, am I going to be next? I'm one of three Blacks on the Senior Tour. I want you to come down here for the funeral and drive back up with me."

"Sure, no problem," I said. "I can see you still hate to fly."

"Clancy, I hate getting airsick, it's embarrassing. I also want you to snoop around here and see what you can find out from the police. You know, use your sources."

"No problem Long Ball, I can do that for you."

"Do you still know that police officer at the Palo Alto Police Department?"

"Who, Tanya Jones?"

"Of course."

"Boy Long Ball, it's been a long time since I talked to her."

"You really liked her, didn't you?"

"Long Ball don't go there. You know how I feel about Tanya." She is one of the most beautiful women I have ever met. We met in college after I got out of the Marines and my tour in the first Gulf War. We got very close.

"Hey Clancy, still there?" asked Long Ball.

"Yes, Long Ball, why did you have to bring her back up?"

"Sorry my brother, I know you must be having some flashbacks about Tanya?"

"You know that's right," I said.

"Long Ball, you know I am still in love with her. But it is over between us."

"When is the last time you spoke to her Clancy?"

"It's been about ten years."

"That's a long time. How was it?"

"Not too bad, I was still upset with her."

"You can't let it go can you Clancy?'

"Long Ball she jilted me. You should know, you were my best man. I still haven't gotten over her. That's why I'm still single. I can't trust women. I will call her when I get down there; only as a favor to you and it will be all professional," I said.

"Yeah right. We'll see how long you can stay professional," Long Ball said laughing.

"Has your brother made any arrangements yet?" I asked.

"He's working on it. We will probably have the services either Thursday or Friday," he said.

"We want to give the family in Atlanta time to get out here," he explained.

Tommy, Long Ball's brother, lives in the San Francisco Bay Area, in Sausalito. He's the president of an advertising agency. As a matter of fact, he has helped Long Ball get some decent endorsements with some major companies.

"When are you going to leave Clancy?" asked Long Ball.

"I'll fly out Monday. Can you pick me up?"

"Of course, you can stay at my place. Unless you want to stay at Tanya's?" Long Ball asked as he laughed again.

"Great, I will see you on Monday," I said.

"Thanks, give the boys my best," Long Ball said.

"Take care bro, bye."

I had to gather my composure before I went back inside the clubhouse. First it was Nina's murder, and now the thought of seeing Tanya again was bringing back all sorts of memories. Tanya was so fine. We were a perfect fit for each other, like hand and glove. I never met anyone like Tanya. No one knew me the way she did and made me feel the way that she could. She completed me.

As I opened the door Ray shouted, "Hey Clancy, you better get your backside in here if you want to get your money!"

"Is everybody through playing?" I asked.

"Yup, get your butt in here!" Ray yelled.

Walking inside the guys could tell that something was wrong. I wasn't looking forward to telling them about Nina. As I walked pass the tables of other players, a waitress was bringing food orders while another waitress was bringing pitchers of beer. You could smell burgers cooking on the grill and fries cooking in the deep-fat fryer.

The clubhouse looked like most others with pictures on the walls of famous golfers of the past and present. Pictures of Ben Hogan, Tiger Woods, Jack Nicholas, Arnold Palmer, Gary Player, Tom Watson, and even Al 'Long Ball' Jackson. On another wall was a picture of Phil Mickelson putting on the Green Jacket from his 2004 win at the Masters by Mike Weir. There were about twenty guys who showed up to play today. It was a good outing.

"What took you so long Clancy? You cleaned up today my brother," Wade Miller said.

"There is about $150.00 in the pot Clancy, and it is all yours," said Jim.

"Hey guys, that was Long Ball on the phone. He called to tell me about his niece, Nina. Nina was murdered." A hush came over the entire clubhouse and tears started to well up in Ray's eyes and several of the other guys as well. Many of the guys worked with Nina when she was in Pinewood's junior golf program.

"Hey look, it's on the news!" Henry yelled.

Julie Monroe, the anchor for Channel-6 News came on to say, "The body of Spokane's very own Nina Jackson was found early this morning at Wild Creek Golf Course in Palo Alto, California. Manuel Garcia, a greens keeper for Wild Creek, found Nina Jackson's body on the ninth green. Let's go live to Wild Creek and get more on the story from Nancy Hampton with our NBC affiliate in Palo Alto," the news anchor said.

"That's right Julie, Nina Jackson's body was found this morning by Manuel Garcia, a grounds keeper at Wild Creek as he was preparing the course for the golfers."

"Mr. Garcia, what did you see this morning?" Nancy Hampton asked.

"I was coming up to the green to start mowing when I saw a body over by the flag. I started yelling for them to wake up. Since we are so close to the railroad tracks, we sometimes get transients on the course sleeping off their last bottle of Thunderbird Wine. Part of our job is to get them off the course before we open. Sometimes we have to call the cops. I didn't think anything of it until I climbed off my mower and reached down to wake the person up. When I pulled the cover back, I saw blood. Her face was completely smashed in and covered in blood.

"Thank you, Mr. Garcia, for that information," Nancy Hampton said.

"Nancy, what have the police said about the case? Do they have any leads or suspects?" Julie asked.

"Julie, I have here with me Detective Tanya Jones, with the Palo Alto Police Department. Detective Jones, is there any correlation with this murder and the other murders of the three other black golfers?"

"I can't comment on that until we examine all the evidence," Detective Jones said.

"Do you have any idea who would do this?" asked Nancy Hampton.

"All I can say is that we are working on this case, and we will keep you informed, thank you."

"Thank you, Detective Jones."

"There you have it Julie, reporting live from Wild Creek Golf Course in Palo Alto,

California, I'm Nancy Hampton for Action Two News."

"We will have more news about the murder of Nina Jackson; please watch Live at Eleven tonight for more details. This has been a Special Report from Channel-6 News."

Everyone in the clubhouse sat there completely stunned at the news. Oh, my god, I saw Tanya. She looked as good as ever. She's a detective now. Seeing Tanya on TV like that brought back so many memories. We were so good together. Tanya had those doe-like brown eyes that always made my knees weak when I looked into them. And just for a moment, I saw a glimpse of her eyes that reminded me of the way we were. How many times did I stare in awe of her and her beauty? We knew what each other was thinking even before we said anything. No one has ever affected me the way that she did. We were so connected. Because of her, my life has never been the same. And because of Nina's death, I'm going to have to see her again and open up old wounds.

"Earth to Clancy, come in Clancy, come back!" Wade shouted.

"Huh? What's up?"

"You're what's up!" yelled Melvin.

"Hey guys, I'm sorry." I looked around the room and saw grown men sobbing. Nina was a special girl. She touched everyone who came in contact with her. Now she's gone. It looked as if

24

everyone was reflecting on their own personal time they shared with Nina. She went from a gangly twelve-year old girl to a beautiful woman of twenty. Some of us spent a lot of time grooming her. But no one was as close to her as her Uncle Al.

Long Ball really helped her through some tough times; especially when her mother died during her junior year in high school. Her dad remarried two years ago: to a beautiful woman named Brenda.

The head pro came over to the table to offer his condolences and express his sorrow at the loss of Nina. The crowded clubhouse got quiet. Guys tallying up their scores and others playing cards sat in stunned silence. It's not very often that someone from this town makes national headlines, especially the murder of a local sports celebrity. Sure, we got our fair share of people who make it big in sports, like John Stockton who played with the Utah Jazz. But nobody affected the community more than Nina and Long Ball. Nina captured the hearts of so many. She had a presence that radiated from her. It became evident when she was crowned Lilac Queen a couple of years ago. Nina was the first African American to be named Lilac Queen in Spokane. She had such poise and gracefulness. During her coronation speech, she expressed her feelings in front of the press, the TV and to everyone. Nina thanked her Lord and Savior Jesu

Christ for giving her this opportunity to serve and represent God and this city.

People were completely overwhelmed by her sincerity and her compassion. She helped break down the walls of racism and bigotry in this city. That's why some of the white people in the clubhouse were crying too.

Normally, I would be rubbing the Pinewood guys' noses in it to let them know how much money I took from them. Not today, however. We're always jawing with each other and talking smack. Now with all this mess going on with Nina, the joy is all gone.

"How's Long Ball doing Clancy?" asked Leonard.

"He's pretty shook up, just like the rest of us. He wants me to fly down on Monday and drive back up with him," I said.

"How long are you going to be down there?" Leonard asked.

"Probably until after the funeral," I told him.

"When's the funeral?" he asked.

"Next Thursday or Friday. Why all the questions Leonard?"

"I just want to know, I'm sure some of the guys would like to attend. If they can't make it, at least we can pitch in on a wreath or something from Pinewood," he said.

"Yeah, I suppose you're right," I told him.

There's always been something a little off about Leonard. I don't know what it is, but there is something different about him. I just can't put my finger on it just yet. All I know, he is a different duck. He's only been with the group for about a year. He's like a gnat always buzzing around you. You want to smack him to get him out of your hair. I have always dreaded that I might get paired up with him. Leonard always wants to give you advice on what you should do on your next shot. Leonard wants to give you pointers as if he's such a great player. Everyone calls him, 'Mr. Know-It-All.' With an eighteen handicap, he's got a lot of nerve telling people what to do. I'm a six, and if I tell him anything he gets angry. I don't understand it. I know Wade wants to smack him upside his head.

"Leonard, why don't you shut up and take your sorry black ass out of here!" shouts Wade.

"Go to hell Wade!" Leonard yelled back.

"Keep it up Leonard, just keep it up. Your day is coming!" Wade warned.

Leonard is about 5'7" and suffers from short-man syndrome. He is constantly trying to get into everyone's Kool-Aid. He's got to know everything, and he thinks he's an expert on every subject. I remember the first time Leonard came out to play with Pinewood last year. The first time anyone comes out to play with the group, it is by invitation only. Jamie Ellis left a message on the hotline saying that he would be bringing

27

his cousin from Alabama. This boy was dressed up like a Black Payne Stewart. He had knickers, a hat, and a sweater vest with the colors of the Atlanta Falcons football team. The late professional golfer Payne Stewart would wear golf outfits that represented one of the NFL football teams at every tournament. Payne's outfit was color-coordinated with the team colors and logo. He set a high standard. Now, this little cocky brother who thinks he can play golf is all dressed up with no place to go. Unfortunately, I ended up having Leonard and Jamie play with my group. Jamie is cool. I've played with him lots of times. I just don't see how Jamie and Leonard are from the same gene pool. Leonard was talking all sorts of garbage about how he was going to take my money. I just came up to the tee and let my driver do the talking. I had a perfect shot, about 247 yards right down the middle of the fairway. Here comes Leonard with his snazzy outfit and his 'Big Bertha' driver. I could tell what was going to happen just by the way he addressed the ball. His hands were open and so was his stance. But lo and behold he didn't slice the ball, he hit a worm burner, barely skipping off the ground that went about 30 yards off the to the right. This whole fiasco went on for five holes. Poor Leonard didn't hit a good drive until the sixth hole. Leonard finally put everything together. He ended up getting his first par and I got a bogey. Would you believe he was all over me for my bogey? This jackass starts telling me what I should do on my next shot. Never mind that I'm even with my birdie on number two and this idiot is eight over after six holes. Leonard's going around thinking like he's all that.

Since Mr. Know-It-All won the last hole, he's first up on number seven, which is a dogleg left with water on the right. I just sat back and watched the boy wonder hit two tee shots right into the water. This was the first time I ever saw someone destroy a $300 driver across their knee. It was like he was possessed. Leonard didn't realize what he did until he reached into his bag to pull out his driver on number nine. Number eight was a short par three, about 142 yards and there he used his eight-iron.

"Hey guys, have you seen my driver?" he asked.

"Leonard, you threw it into the garbage can back on seven," I said.

"What do you mean, I left my driver at seven? Take me back there!" he shouted in disbelief.

Leonard and Jamie drove their golf cart back down through the winding cart path to the seventh tee to get the remnants of his 'Big Bertha' driver. Wade and I like to walk the course when we play. Walking gives you time to think and helps you prepare for your next shot. While cart golf always makes me feel like I am rushing to hit the ball.

We had to let the group behind us play through so we wouldn't hold up play and have the course marshal breathing down our necks. I could hear Leonard swearing as they were driving back towards us as he realized what he had done. It was at that moment that I knew Leonard was a couple of cards short of a full deck. After they got back from their excursion and got out of the cart to join us, I noticed Leonard reaching into his golf bag. He popped a couple of pills from a prescription bottle into his mouth. I had no idea what he took. All I know, he appeared to mellow out on the back nine. From fifteen on, Leonard was halfway decent. He got pars on 15, 16, and bogeys on 17 and 18. If you know how to deal with him, he's not a bad guy. However, if he's not caught up on his meds, watch out.

Leonard shot a 97, Jamie an 84, Wade an 81, and me, a 78. The way Leonard was talking, he acted like he was the one that got the best score. And sure enough, the guys got on him about breaking his driver. Leonard's been an irritation ever since that first day. I'm glad that Archie was there to keep Leonard from getting his teeth knocked down his throat.

A bunch of guys were going down to Murphy's Red Lion for some BBQ and drinks. It sounded like a good idea. I could bump my gums on some ribs and wine broiled chicken. Murphy's is our main watering hole that we usually go to after a round of golf. Now, depending on what time we finish playing, we may get there as early as 1:00 in the afternoon or as late as 6:30. Either way, some of these guys start drinking pretty hard once they get to Murphy's; me included.

Pete Williams, the pro at Diamondback came over to talk to me some more about Nina.

"Clancy, have you talked to Long Ball?" he asked.

"Yes, I just got off the phone with him," I said.

"How's he doing?"

"Considering the circumstances, he's holding up well," I told him.

"When's the funeral?"

"Probably this Thursday or Friday," I said.

"Are you going?"

"Yes, as a matter of fact I'm leaving on Monday."

"Pete, I want to thank you for letting us play here this weekend."

Since Diamondback is a private course, they generally don't open it up to the public. But since Long Ball and I are members, they decided to let Pinewood play this weekend only. Long Ball and I are among five Black members of this club.

"Clancy, that's another reason I want to talk to you. Some of our members are complaining about your group's behavior," he said.

"What do you mean by our behavior?" I asked.

"Well, you know?"

"No, I don't know! You better explain what you're talking about," I said shaking my head in disbelief.

"Well, you know, you people don't act like we do on the course," he said.

"Tell me Pete, how should we act?" I asked.

"You always seem to be arguing, shouting and carrying on all the time," he said.

"Do you really believe we are acting any different than the white players here?"

"Clancy, I'm sorry, but I just want you to know what I am hearing from the other members. Let's face it, if it wasn't for Long Ball, you wouldn't be a member," he said arrogantly.

"Pete, you know if it wasn't for your father, who adopted you, and with Long Ball's help, you wouldn't be here either," I said.

Long Ball and Danny Williams, Pete's father, were instrumental in Pete getting this job at Diamondback.

It seems like only yesterday that Danny Williams and Long Ball were the last twosome on the final day of the U.S. Senior Open, which was three years ago. Danny had a three-shot lead over Long Ball going into the Par-4 16th. Danny's tee shot is usually straight as an arrow; he hooked it into the evergreen trees at Sunset Shores in Portland, Oregon. Danny had to pitch it back out onto the fairway because his ball was behind a tree. Unfortunately, he didn't hit it all the way into the fairway and got into the first cut of rough. Because of this, the club got hung up in the deep grass and caused his ball to go into the green side bunker. Danny, a great sand player, pitched out of the sand and landed his ball three feet from the pin. It was a spectacular shot but now he only had a two-stroke lead with his bogey putt.

Long Ball on the other hand had a superb drive; 270 yards right down the middle of the fairway. With 185 yards to the pin, Long Ball reached the green with his 6-iron and had a 12-foot birdie putt. He landed on the upper tier of the undulating green. If he makes this putt, it would be a two-shot swing for him, and Danny would only have a one-stroke lead going into the Par-3 17th.

Long Ball's putt slowed down as it died at the hole and as if one final plea, which seemed like an eternity; the ball went in. A loud roar of applause came forth from the gallery.

Danny glanced over to Long Ball and gave him a nod acknowledging his great putt. Long Ball is back in the hunt.

The 17th is a long 202-yard par three with an elevated green, surrounded by water on both sides.

I always told Long Ball that when he makes it to the Senior Tour, I want to be his caddie. It was a wonderful feeling to be at a major tournament and feel all the excitement in the air. And, to watch history being made at the U.S. Senior Open with Danny Williams and Al 'Long Ball' Jackson going head-to-head was incredible. After watching Long Ball sink that birdie putt; knowing that he may have a chance to win this tournament was awesome.

There was a hush over the crowd as Long Ball addressed the ball. He picked his four-iron. His swing is a thing of beauty. I have always tried to emulate him. He brought the club back low and slow with a perfect shoulder and hip rotation. His body coiled up at the peak of his back swing. Long Ball unleashed all his energy from his body and club into the golf ball and it exploded off the clubface as if it was launched out of a cannon.

I have never seen him hit such a beautiful shot. The ball went right over the flag and landed five feet from the pin. The backspin on the ball and the slope of the green brought it back within four inches from the hole. The crowd started shouting, "Long Ball! Long Ball! You're the man!" It was deafening.

The pressure was now on Danny Williams. What would he do? He had to get a par at least to

34

keep it even. He needs to make this birdie. The past three days he went par, birdie, and birdie. Danny's tee shot was gorgeous. He was pin-high with an easy six-foot putt.

The crowd was elated as they both approached the green. You could hear a pin drop while everyone waited for Danny to sink his putt. Danny's putt looked as if it was going to go straight in. It broke a little to the right, caught the edge of the cup, and did an infamous horseshoe. It lipped out. He missed an opportunity to keep his lead. Danny was still away and had to make his one-foot putt. He tapped in for par, while Long Ball tapped in for a birdie and his share of the lead at 9-under. Both have a7 shot lead over Rich Allen who finished with a 68 and had third place all to himself.

The Par-5 18th is the longest hole on the course and the toughest at 610 yards. Water comes into play on this menacing hole on both sides of the fairway. There is water that hugs the left side of the fairway with intermittent trees about 270 yards. It continues across the fairway onto the right side all along the base of the hill to this treacherous elevated green.

You need to have a good drive between 250 and 275 yards. This still leaves you with a long second shot, which will set you up with a nice approach shot to the green. Course management is critical on this hole. Many a tournament has been won or lost on number 18. They call it

'Hamburger Hill,' because it will grind you up to a pulp if you don't play it right.

Your third shot will leave you with a 165-yard shot to the green if you play it smart. However, it is uphill and you're going in blind. This hole is unique. A monitor is at the base of the slope alongside the cart path.

If you are 165 yards out, you will have a blind shot and you can't see the flag. Some people will judge their shot just before they lose the view of the pin placement. Others use the monitor, both work well. However, if you miss the green or the ball doesn't stick. The ball dribbles back down the hill about fifty feet until the ball is stopped by the long rough, giving you a tough uphill shot.

There are three sand traps surrounding the green. There is one on each side and one at the back. Either way, if you're not careful, you'll get into big trouble.

It's white-knuckle time for Danny Williams and Long Ball. Two of the best players on the Senior Tour are coming down to the wire. Long Ball is first up. I don't know if it is best to tee off first to set the pace, and put pressure on Danny, or see what your opponent is going to do. Will he hit a great tee shot, or hit an errant shot and open the door for you? Long Ball's shot was perfect, it went left-center in the fairway and long, about 272 yards. He can lay up with a 3-

iron or a fairway wood and be in good position to get on in three.

Danny's drive was just as good and went about eight yards farther than Long Ball's. Both were smiling nervously as they were walking towards their golf balls; wondering what to do for their next shot. They both knew that they had to play these next shots perfectly.

Everything is coming down to the wire right here. This could be Danny Williams' second win and his first back-to-back U.S. Senior Open title. And Long Ball could be the first African American to win a U.S. Senior Open title. You couldn't ask for a better finish. Would they tie? Would there be a playoff? If they did, they would play another 18 holes the next day.

It has been four grueling days and from the looks on both of their faces, they would love to get it over with right now.

Since Long Ball was away, he was first up. Instead of going with his three-wood, he went with his five-wood. He knew that he had better control with his five. It was a great second shot, about 205 yards, right at the base of the hill. He's going to have to use the monitor for his approach shot.

I don't know what's gotten into Danny, it must be the adrenaline. He used his driver and got all of it. He got so much of it that the ball looked like it was going to go into the water. At the last minute, it just shot straight up and out as it hit a rock on the bank of the creek, which launched it into the side of the hill into the rough. After Long Ball walked up to his ball, he looked at the monitor, made his calculations, stepped up to the ball, and hit a beautiful 8-iron about ten feet from the pin. Danny was very frustrated with his last shot. He was so deep in the rough there wasn't much he could do. He took his 9-iron hoping to get enough of the club on the ball to keep the head from turning. Danny did the best he could, and it looked like it was going to work. Unfortunately, it hit the slope on the fringe of the green and rolled back into the first cut of rough. It was sitting up and you could tell it was going to be a flyer. He pulled out his sand-wedge and tried to lob it thirty yards onto the green. Danny didn't have a lot of green to work with and the ball flew over the flag into the back bunker. The three worse words in golf are, "You're still away." Danny saw the tournament slip away through his fingers. He's shooting five to get out of the sand trap and hopefully, he can still salvage a bogey. Sure enough, Danny came within three feet of the cup. Knowing that all Long Ball had to do was make a par for the win. Danny putted and made his bogey. Long Ball had a testy ten-footer. Sometimes the hardest part is knowing that all you need to do is make one of these last two putts to win.

I could tell Long Ball was nervous. Millions of people were watching this putt from all over the world. Long Ball was like the Mohammed Ali of golf. Long Ball knew the minute he hit the ball it was off. He stubbed his putter on the ground before he hit the ball. It only went four feet. The crowd groaned when they saw what happened. You never want to leave yourself short. Danny perked up when he realized he still might have a chance for a playoff. To say the least, this six-foot putt would be the most important putt in Long Ball's life. Long Ball, being the champion that he is, dug down deep to get himself focused. He looked as if he was possessed. You knew without a doubt that this ball was going to go in. Sure enough, the ball went in as if a laser was guiding it right into the center of the cup.

Long Ball dropped to his knees and began to sob. Everyone was applauding and shouting for Long Ball. In a true form of sportsmanship, Danny Williams came over and extended his hand to Long Ball to help him get back up on his feet. Both players embraced and congratulated each other for a great tournament. From that day on Long Ball's career took off. Danny's on the other hand was never the same again. I feel that Danny's son has never forgiven Long Ball for beating his father. It's really sad.

CHAPTER TWO

GIVE ME MY SHOT

Some of the guys got there ahead of me and were nursing their drinks. Murphy yelled out, "Hey Clancy, what are you having today?"

"After all that has gone on today, I think I'll have a shot of Jack Daniels, make it neat," I said.

"What's got your panties all knotted up Clancy?" Murphy asked. "Didn't play well today, eh?"

"Actually, I played great. I shot a 74." I told him.

"Then what's the problem?" inquired Murphy.

I don't know if I should tell him about Pete or tell him about Nina. Murphy made it easy for me.

"It must be Nina," he said. "Wade told me the news when he came in. It's a real shame, she was such a sweet girl."

"Yes, that's part of it," I told him.

"Why don't you give me my shot and keep them coming. Maybe that will loosen up my tongue and you'll get more information out of me," I said.

"What else is on your mind Clancy? I haven't seen you like this since you and Tanya broke up."

"Boy, does it show that much?" I asked.

"It's all over your face," he said.

"There are some other things that have gotten me all riled up."

"Like what Clancy?"

"Do you know Pete Williams, the Pro at Diamondback?"

"Yeah, Karen's brother. I know that spoiled little puke. He's come in here a few times. Boy, you should hear him talk about you and the Pinewood guys."

"Like what?"

"Pete was here about a month or so ago. He had a few drinks, and he started to spout off about the Pinewood guys. Saying that he is so glad not to be working at the Canyon so he wouldn't have to put up with the darkies any longer. Clancy, I wanted to punch him so bad."

"Murphy, you would have done me a favor. I almost decked him today. He started going off on me this afternoon about us playing out there today. He was saying that the members didn't like the way we were acting on the course. You know, we are just like any of the other golfers out there playing. We want to have fun and enjoy ourselves on the course.

And I've seen a lot of white players drunk and obnoxious at Diamondback. I wonder if they get any complaints from the good ole boys at the club?"

"I doubt it, my friend."

"Doggone it Murphy, I get so frustrated with this crap. It sure doesn't look like it's going to get any better with all these Black golfers getting killed.

"Do you wonder who the next one might be Clancy?" Murphy asked.

"Yes, I do Murphy. Yes, I do."

"You want another shot Clancy?"

"I sure do, keep them coming."

I took my drink and went over to the table where Wade and some of the other guys were sitting. They were tanked already. I suppose if I keep drinking Jack Daniels, I will catch up with them.

Wade hollered over to Karen the waitress, "Bring us another round of drinks and make Clancy's a double!"

"I don't know that is a good idea Wade, I got an early flight in the morning."

"Shut up Clancy, you need it," Wade slurred.

The problem is these drinks are going down way too easy. I'm not even getting drunk from all the alcohol. I must be numb, I thought to myself. I was hoping that the alcohol would help me forget everything. But my mind kept flashing back to Tanya. How will I react when I see her again? I was so hurt for what she did to me. I told myself that I would not allow anyone to get that close to me again. I know that Long Ball wants me to go down to California and protect him. However, I need to find out what we are up against. That means I must see Tanya and try to persuade her to share with me any evidence she might have on Nina's murder and the others.

"It's about time you brought us our drinks," Wade said to Karen.

Karen came over and sat down next to me for a minute.

"Clancy, I'm sorry to hear about Nina," she said.

"Thanks Karen, it's hard to believe that she's gone. How could someone do that to her?"

"There are some crazy people out there Clancy, no one is safe anymore," she said.

"Karen, order up!" Barney yelled from the kitchen.

As Karen got up from the table she asked, "Clancy, do want something to eat?"

"Yeah, I better."

"The Bobby Special?" she asked.

The Bobby Special is one-half pound of ribs, and one-quarter pound of chicken.

"You know what I always order."

"Fries, or baked beans?"

"Fries with beans on the side," I said.

"Wine broiled, or BBQ chicken?"

43

"Wine broiled."

Karen looked at me and said, "If you need anything else and I do mean anything else, call me. You still have my number, don't you?"

"Yes Karen, I still have your number," I whispered.

She winked at me and went off to get the order from Barney.

"What's that all about Clancy?" Wade asked.

"Nothing at all."

"Are you getting some of that Clancy?"

"No Wade, we are just good friends."

"Clancy, good friends don't give you those bedroom green eyes that she is flashing your way my brother."

"Is it that obvious?" I asked.

"Clancy, she's doing everything but tucking you into bed."

"Wade, I can't."

"Keep on drinking and I bet you will."

Let me see. How long has it been since I was with Karen? I asked myself. It must be close to three years. I didn't even think about being with Karen again until Wade asked me. We had a very physical relationship, but it was always kept hush, hush. We didn't want anyone to find out, especially her brother Pete Williams, the golf pro at Diamondback. Karen was a good friend. We were there for each other if we needed someone to talk to. You know, she is that one person you can talk to about all your dirt?

Dirt that you've been keeping to yourself and nobody else knows but that one special friend. Well, Karen is that one friend. The chemistry has always been there between us, but she was concerned about what her family would say if she dated a Black man. She wasn't worried about her parents; she was more concerned about her brother and her uncle, Doug Spencer. He is Karen's uncle on her mother's side. Doug is from Little Rock, Arkansas. He was stationed at Fairchild Air Force Base and decided to stay in Spokane when he retired in 2000. He spent thirty years in the service.

"Here you go sweetie," Karen said as she put the tray of food on the table.

"Thanks Karen."

"Can I get you fellows anything else?"

"No thanks Karen."

She took off and went to deliver an order to another customer. Wade reached over and nearly burned his fingers as he grabbed one of my ribs.

"Did you burn yourself? Serves you right; you wretch. How can you reach over and grab my food without asking me? Didn't your momma teach you any manners boy?"

"Don't go talking about my momma," he said laughing.

"You want some fries?"

"Thanks."

45

"Clancy, look who just walked in," Wade said.

I looked up and to my surprise it was Pete.

"Man, of all the people I did not want to see tonight was Pete. He just ruined my meal. He's got a lot of nerve to show up here after what he said to me in the clubhouse."

Pete saw me as he came in and he had that cocky look on his face. He knows he is goading me.

"I ought to go over there and deck that sorry piece of crap," I said to Wade.

"Clancy, do you feel like spending the night in jail?" Wade asked.

"No not tonight, he's lucky I'm leaving tomorrow, otherwise I would deck that punk."

"He's such a worm. Pete didn't have to work for anything. His daddy gave him everything Wade."

"Yeah, I know."

"Clancy, what time are you leaving tomorrow?"

"Damn it Wade, I forgot to make my reservations! I better call Southwest Airlines."

As I was getting up to go outside, I made eye contact with Pete. I could feel my blood pressure begin to rise. He had a smug look on his face. The night air was warm and there was still a gentle breeze. It felt good to get out of the bar and the smoke. The traffic was light on Division for a Sunday evening but wait until tomorrow

46

morning and it is going to be bumper-to-bumper. I can't believe how this city has grown. Let me see if I still have Southwest's number programmed in my cell phone. Let's see, I punched 'S' on my keypad. I had to scroll down past Sarah and Sue before I got to SWA for Southwest Airlines. I hit the phone icon.

"Thank you for calling Southwest Airlines, this is Mary, may I help you?"

"Yes Mary, I need to get a one-way ticket to San Jose. What is the earliest flight you have available?"

"I have flight 1130 that leaves at 6:05 and arrives at 10:30 after making two stops. And I have another one that leaves Spokane at 7:20 and gets in at 11:50 with 1 stop."

"Mary, I'll take the 7:20."

I gave Mary my credit card information and went back inside the bar. To my surprise, I saw Leonard talking to Pete. What in the world would those two have in common?

"Wade, how long have those two been talking?"

"Ever since you went outside Clancy. They look pretty friendly too."

"For a guy that doesn't seem to like Black folks too much, he sure seems to be best buds with Leonard," I said.

"What do you make of that Clancy?"

"Wade, all I can say is, watch your back."

"You got that right. What time are you leaving tomorrow?"

"I'm leaving at 7:20."

"What are going to do about Karen?"

"Man, why are you bringing that up?"

"Because Karen's got those bedroom eyes for you. What kind of spell do you have on her man?"

"Wade, she's a great friend."

"That's not all. Here she comes Clancy. Hey Karen, Clancy wants you to take him home."

"Are you having too much fun here tonight, or do you want to have some special fun?" she said with a sexy smile.

"Clancy, for a high yellow, Black man, I do believe you are turning red my brother."

"Wade, do you know you can be a real ass?"

"Well Clancy, what are you going to do? Karen asked.

"Bring me another shot of Jack and I will let you know."

"What are you saying? That you got to be drunk to be with me?"

"No Karen, it just makes it easier," I said with a straight face.

I caught her left hand just as she was about to slap me. I kissed the back of her hand and turned that frown into a suggestive smile. I know the alcohol must be taking over any type of right reasoning I may have had has now left me. It's been a long time and Karen is one fine woman.

"That's better Clancy, you better treat me right if you want to get some," Karen said as she walked off to get another order from the kitchen.

"Wade, I'm going to kill your sorry ass."

"Clancy, would you rather be with me or Karen?"

"Well, you are cute, but I'm not that kind of guy. Although there is nothing wrong with that type of behavior, however, if I was that type of guy, you would be the one for me."

"Gee whiz Clancy, I can't tell you how wonderful that makes me feel. I'm touched. You sure you don't want to come home with me instead?"

"Without a doubt."

We continued with our meal and had a few more drinks.

"I don't know about you Wade, I'm stuffed, and I got a great buzz going on."

"I know what you mean, I'm pretty hammered myself."

Wade reached into his back pocket and pulled out a bag of chewing tobacco. After taking some out, he passed it over to me.

"You want some Clancy?" he asked as he shoved a big wad into his mouth.

"You know Wade, I'm drunk enough to chew on some of this crap."

"Karen ought to love kissing you tonight," Wade said laughing.

I took a wad out and put it in my mouth and packed it on the left side of my cheek.

"The sad thing is Wade; I really do like chewing this stuff. I haven't chewed for quite a while."

I reached over to grab one of the empty beer glasses and spit some juice in it. Wade is one of those guys that will swallow the juice.

"Man, you must have an iron stomach. I don't know how you can do it."

"You get used to it Clancy, believe me, a few times I got sick from swallowing it. Sometimes you're unable to find a place to spit and you just have to swallow it."

It tasted good at first, then after a while my head started to spin a little bit. I don't know if it is from all the booze, food, or a combination of tobacco, it was making me queasy. I had an incredible urge to purge. Wade looked at me and saw that I was turning green. It was almost too late to make it to the head, but fortunately, I found it just in time as the remnants of the Bobby Special was evacuating my stomach. I hate losing it like this. Wade came into the bathroom to check on me to see if I was okay.

"Hey Clancy, you alive in there?"

"Yes, I think so. I believe the worst is over. I don't know what the hell hit me. All of a sudden, I felt this wave of heat and gurgling in

50

my stomach. Next thing I know I'm running in here to kiss the porcelain god."

"Clancy, it's a good thing that Karen's going to give you a ride home. Are you going to leave your car here?"

"No, I don't think so. I'm going to have her drive my car."

When I came out of the bathroom, I could see Pete and Karen talking. It looked like it wasn't a friendly exchange of words between siblings. I started to go over there to see if she needed my help, but she gave me a glance that said to stay clear. Karen's a pretty sharp gal and she knows how to take care of herself. She's got a black belt in Karate and doesn't put up with a lot of crap. I've seen her throw some big dudes out of the bar. She can be rather intimidating with her 5'9" frame. However, she sure knows how to make a pair of Levi's stand out. Karen goes to her dojo at least three times a week and goes to the gym five days a week to lift weights and do aerobics. She's got a hard body that won't quit. I guess it is her great body that's got me all worked up with those long firm legs of hers. A lovely backside that just makes you want to shout! Also, did I mention her strong muscular arms, a 26" rock-hard waist, and the best pair of 38's you've ever seen? What a package. I can't help myself. I started to think how nice it would be to spend the night with her again.

From the looks of their conversation, Pete must be asking her about me. I don't think he has any idea that we use to spend time together. Or does he? Our relationship, if you can call it that, is purely physical. We could always call each other up and either she would come over to my place, or vice versa. We were there for each other. And the beauty of it all, there were no strings attached. I guess you might say it was selfish, but we had an understanding. We both got hurt badly before and we didn't want to make any commitments to expose ourselves.

I could tell that Karen was upset. Her face started to turn red as her hair. She kept her voice down, but you could hear Pete shout as he stormed out the side door of Murphy's, "You stay away from that nigger! You hear me!"

That is the last thing you say when you have ten brothers in here. Wade and I both started to get up, but Karen rushed over to our table to stop us.

"Please Clancy, don't go after him," she said.

"Are you okay?" I asked.

"I'm okay."

"Can you give me about twenty minutes to do my tickets and I will be ready to go?"

"Are you sure, I can have Wade give me a ride?"

I felt an elbow from Wade in my side as I said that. And Karen gave me a look that said, are you crazy?

"Clancy, I don't mind at all. I need someone to talk to anyway."

"Okay, I'll be here."

Karen went upstairs to the office and from where I was sitting, she gave me a great preview of what I would be looking at later in more detail.

CHAPTER THREE

THE SKY IS CRYING

It was good to be outside and get some fresh air. The smell of cigarettes spilled, beer, and BBQ was overwhelming in there. I always love the summer evenings in Spokane. It was still warm at 12 in the morning, about 75 degrees with a slight breeze. The joint was still jumping down at Slow Eddies, which is another bar on the other side of Division Street about a block away. It sounded like someone was playing a Stevie Ray Vaughn tune, 'The Sky is Crying.'

I gave Karen the keys to the Jeep, and she pushed the button on top of the key fob to unlock the doors. Karen opened the passenger door for me and helped me to get in. We were both silent for a few minutes and I had to ask her. "What was that all about with your brother?"

"You don't want to know Clancy."

"The hell I don't!" I shouted.

"Look, your brother has been a real asshole lately and he deserves to get the hell knocked out of him if he doesn't straighten out."

"I know he's been a real jerk," Karen said.

"That's an understatement," I said.

"Clancy, he hasn't been the same since he's been going down to Arkansas."

"What in the world is he doing in Arkansas?" I asked.

"Our uncle lives in Little Rock. He decided to move back down there after living in Spokane for a while. Pete has been spending a lot of time with him."

"So."

"Well, you see, our uncle is racist, and it has rubbed off on Pete."

"What do you mean out there?"

"He's involved with a Neo-Nazi White Supremacist group, and I believe he's been influencing Pete."

"That may explain all these wise ass comments he's been making lately. What's your dad say about it?"

"Dad hasn't been around that much. You know with him being on the tour right now he doesn't have a lot of time to be with us. Plus, I don't think anyone has said anything to him about it yet. I haven't said anything, and I know no one else has talked to Mom."

"Do you think your uncle is filling his head with this white supremacist crap?"

"Without a doubt Clancy. Pete is spending a lot of time with him. There's a group of them that he has met with in Idaho."

55

"How long has that been going on?"

"For about eight months."

"You're kidding me?"

"No, I'm not. I wish I were."

"Wow, that's amazing."

I had to roll down the window to get some fresh air. I couldn't believe what Karen was telling me about her brother. He sounds like he has gone off the deep end. We were getting close to my place. A few more of these winding turns on Upriver Drive and I can get Karen out of her tight jeans. Karen's been over at my house so often I didn't have to tell her to turn right on Windsor Way. I reached over and hit the button on the garage door opener on the driver's side visor while Karen drove the Jeep inside.

"Karen, thanks for driving me home. I don't think I would have made it by myself."

Karen leaned over to me and put her right hand on my thigh and whispered, "You're welcome sweetie."

I grabbed her face with both hands and kissed her on her lips. We both started to get excited, and she motioned for us to go inside. I slid out of my seat and tried to stand up straight once I got out of the Jeep. I felt a little wobbly. Karen came over to help me stand up and walk inside.

"Please push the button on the wall so I can close the garage door," I slurred. We left a trail of clothing from the kitchen where we came in from the garage leading all the way upstairs to my bedroom. Once inside my bedroom, Karen pushed me down onto the bed.

"Get under the covers and I will be right back," she said.

I leaned over and set my alarm clock for 4:30. It was already 1:08. I'm one of those guys who likes to arrive early at the airport. It's going to take me an hour to get ready anyway. I forgot that I still had my shorts on. I could hear the water running in the bathroom as I slid my shorts off. I crawled underneath the covers waiting for Karen to come out. I closed my eyes imagining what would be taking place shortly. Unfortunately, my head started to spin, and I went out. The next thing I heard was the obnoxious buzz from my alarm clock. I fumbled with the clock trying to turn it off. I managed to hit the snooze button so I could stop the buzzing sound. I looked over to my right and Karen was sound asleep. Her long red hair was trying to cover her bare shoulders. I drifted off again and this time I managed to turn off the alarm after the nine-minute grace period was over. Even though I only got a few hours of sleep, I felt like I could perform now. I nudged Karen but to no avail. She was zonked out. With no opportunity looming, I crawled out of bed.

I opened my closet door to grab my white terrycloth robe off the hook that was behind the door. As I walked down the stairs putting on my robe, there were remnants of what could have been. Clothes were scattered all about. My tee shirt was on the landing, while my golf shirt was at the bottom of the stairs. One of my Birkenstocks was on the first step next to Karen's blouse. I found the other one in the kitchen. My head was pounding and there were two things I needed, coffee and Advil. Fortunately, I keep both in the cupboard. After successfully lining up the safety arrows on the cap of the Advil bottle, I flipped off the top. I was going to take three; when I decided I better make it four 200 mg pills. As I went over to the sink and turned the water on, I shoved the four pills in my mouth and bent over to slurp up water with my hand. One of my early action items was complete.

The next thing on my to-do list was coffee. The coffee grinder still had some coffee in it but not enough to make a full pot. I could hear the water running in the background. I suppose I should either turn it off or fill the coffee pot. My mind is functioning like a finely tuned machine, I said to myself. I put enough water in there for six cups. This time I turned off the faucet. Reaching up to the second shelf in the cupboard I found the sealed container that kept my Peet's Coffee fresh. Luckily, there was no safety lid to fumble with. After I filled the grinder with Sumatran coffee beans, I pressed the switch on. I could tell this is not going to be a day for loud noises. While the coffee was brewing, I went

58

back up the stairs picking up our clothes as I came across them. I nudged Karen again; this time she woke up.

"What time is it?" Karen asked.

"It is ten-to-five. I guess I passed out," I said.

"I came out of the bathroom with nothing on and it sounded like you were cutting logs. You were out. I couldn't get you to wake up."

"Do you want to join me in the shower?" I pleaded.

"No, I'm going back to sleep. I'll take Lyft home. I'm tired."

"Hey Karen, I'm sorry about last night. Here's twenty bucks for Lyft" That's not the first time Karen has taken Lyft home from my place. Sometimes if I had an early tee time she would stay and sleep in. Karen would always tidy up the place and make the bed. The shower revitalized me somewhat. The kicker was the coffee. After a couple of cups, I felt energized, but I still had that what have I done hangover feeling. My gear was all packed and I decided to take my Beretta 9-mm just in case. I poured a final cup of coffee into my travel mug to take with me to the airport.

The sun was coming up and it was getting warm at six o'clock already. The temperature gauge inside my Jeep said 69 degrees. As I backed out of the garage, I took a long look at my beautiful house and thought how lucky I was to have this place.

Several years ago, when the housing market was in a slump here in Spokane, I purchased a nice piece of riverfront property in Millwood. Millwood is a suburb of the Spokane Valley. It's a nice older neighborhood with a lot of character. I'm sort of old-fashioned like that, I guess. I built my house like a two-story traditional-style Victorian home with a full basement. It had a complete wrap-around porch with a three-tier deck in the back overlooking the river. There are stairs that lead up to another deck off the master bedroom, which have French Doors instead of a slider for a little added charm. All of this is on a one-acre lot with about 150 feet of waterfront property. It is very relaxing and serene here. Tanya was excited about this house. She was going to turn the house into our home. But that didn't happen.

I took Argonne Road south to Interstate-90 West towards the Spokane International Airport. Along the way, I couldn't stop thinking about Nina. What a waste. I know one thing for sure, I'm going to find him and I'm going to kill him. Is this the same person who is most likely responsible for all the other murders too? Nina's murder has to be linked with all the others. Long Ball must be concerned as well. Are they going to stop, or are they going to keep on killing? I may have to plan a trip down to Oregon to check on the Mackey case. Police departments aren't that willing to give information to private investigators, especially to a former cop.

It was several years ago; five to be exact that my partner and I, Jim Larson, were working undercover on a drug deal. We were all set to go forward with the buy for 2 kilos of Peruvian Flake cocaine. You know what they say, timing is everything. Unfortunately, I recognized one of the men from a previous collar I made 11 years ago, Jonathan Howard. I busted him for possession and distribution of heroin. He had 4 kilos of black tar heroin. It was the biggest undercover sting operation in Spokane's history at the time. Jonathan spent 10 years in Walla-Walla State Penitentiary. I was hoping that he would not recognize me. Unfortunately, I wouldn't be that lucky on that fateful day. Jonathan was a member of the 'Rough Riders' motorcycle gang. Jonathan was responsible for supplying drugs throughout the entire region east of the Cascades down to the Yakima Valley, Tri-Cities, Eastern Oregon, and Montana better known as the Inland Empire. My beard was not that good enough of a disguise to fool him.

He said, "I know you man, you look real familiar."

I reached out my hand to shake his and told him, "I'm Billy Anderson." He didn't grab my hand. I glanced over at Jim behind me, and I could tell he was getting nervous. He was sitting at the table with some guy named Ricky.

Ricky had a .357 on the table, which was within easy reach if needed.

"Man, I know you from somewhere," Jonathan said.

"I'm sorry, this is the first time I've ever seen you," I said. I hope he believes this lie, I thought to myself. If not, something bad is going to happen.

"Hey, have you ever been in the joint?" Jonathan asked.

"Of course, I have. I was in McNeil Island back in 2004. I got out in 2009. I did five years for dealing."

Jonathan looked at me and asked. "Did you know Angelo Martino? He was a good friend of mine. We did a lot of business on the outside."

"Yeah, he was in E Block I think." As soon as I said I knew him, I saw him reach for his gun. I was doing the same thing. Ricky had his .357 poised at the right side of Jim's head.

"Billy, if that is your real name? You're a lying bastard!" shouted Jonathan. "There was no Angelo Martino in McNeil. He's, my attorney!"

It was a Mexican standoff. We had guns trained on each other, except for Jim. He didn't have time to pull out his weapon.

"Drop it or your friend gets it!" he yelled.

"No fricking way!" I shouted back at him.

"You better drop it!" shouted Jonathan.

"Don't do it Clancy!" Jim shouted.

Ricky pistol-whipped Jim and he crumpled down to the floor.

"For the last time, put your gun down. Or I'm going to put a hole in your partner's head!"

All I could do was remember what my instructor said at the academy. "Under no circumstances give up your weapon." Here I am, I have no choice. Jim was waking up. I decided to drop my gun. Just as soon as my weapon hit the ground Ricky pulled the trigger on his .357. Blood started gushing out of the hole on the right side of Jim's head.

Jonathan was yelling at Ricky, "Why the hell did you do that!"

I dove over the sofa onto the floor and grabbed my .38 that I had strapped to my leg under my pants. I fired a head shot back at Ricky splattering blood and pieces of his brain against the window as he collapsed to the floor. Jonathan ran out the door with one other guy involved in the buy. Fortunately, we were wired, and both guys ran into our backup outside who shot them both. One of them died instantly. The other is confined to a wheelchair and the walls of Walla-Walla State Penitentiary for life.

All hell broke loose after Jim's death. "I had no choice but to give up my gun," I said to Internal Affairs investigators. They didn't see it that way. I kept arguing why didn't our backup get in there in time.

"No one could give me an answer." The investigator said, "We wanted to make sure that the buy was going to happen."

But for some reason, they couldn't react fast enough to come in when they knew we were cops. Jim and I had been partners for six years. We worked well together. His wife Mary was very understanding. However, his dad, Lieutenant Mark Larson, held me responsible and was instrumental in getting me kicked off the force. I was devastated. Being a cop was my whole life, just like my dad.

Once I got on I-90 West it was only 23 minutes to the airport. It was supposed to warm up to 85 today. The sun was starting to rise and cast long morning shadows behind me. The traffic was relatively light except for the eighteen-wheelers that were either just starting their morning runs or just finishing up their nightshift hauls by heading to the truck stops off Highway 2. Interstate-90 cuts right through the heart of Spokane. Traffic is always a nightmare off the north and south main corridors. Monroe and Division Streets are so congested that the city has one of the highest particulate counts in the country. Perhaps one of these days they will have a north/south freeway completed to alleviate the congestion and pollution.

As I got closer, I could see planes taking off from Spokane International Airport. I took the airport exit and I could tell that the people who were doing 90 mph were going to be late for their flight. I just cruised by at 65 and sure enough, the Washington State Highway Patrol was there waiting for them. No doubt they will be taking a later flight. I went up to curbside check-in to drop off my bags before I parked. I hate hauling my luggage and golf clubs. Luckily, my skycap buddy Phil was working today, and I could drop my stuff off and he would have me all squared away after I parked.

"Hey Phil, how's it going?" I asked.

"Not too bad Clancy, where are you heading"? Phil asked.

"I'm going down to the Bay Area, flying into San Jose to meet Al Jackson. I'm going to Nina Jackson's funeral service."

"I'm sorry to hear about Nina, that's a shame that some nut did that to her," he said.

"It sure is," I said.

"Are you going to do a little snooping around?"

Phil and I go back a long way. We're old ski buddies and he knows that I am a private detective. He's a good source too. He knows a lot of people around town. He has a good ear for what's happening on the street.

"Yeah, I'm going to try to check things out. Hey, let me go to the garage and park my car. I'll be right back."

"No problem, Clancy, see in a few."

65

I pulled up to the gate at the entrance to the parking garage and heard 'Pollyanna' say, "Please take the ticket." Once the gate went up. I was on my way up the spiral ramp to the top deck. Every level I passed said full. So, my last resort was the top where my Jeep would be exposed to the elements. Needless to say, I will no doubt have a message written in the dust saying, "Please wash me." I grabbed my backpack off the passenger seat and headed down the five flights of stairs. I figure I better see if I can shake loose this hangover. The idea of going down the elevator made my stomach queasy. I crossed the street and went over to get my baggage claim tickets from Phil.

"Clancy, you're all set. You're at the B Concourse at Gate 7."

"Thanks, Phil. Hey, how's that restaurant opportunity looking for you?"

"Actually, things are looking pretty good. I got several investors lined up. All we need to do is find the right location."

"Glad to hear it. It's about time you got your own place. You put Murphy's ribs to shame.

"Make sure you make it to the lake this summer," Phil said.

"You can count on it. See you later." Phil's a great guy. He's got a catering business he does on the side. He pulls around this barbeque setup to state and county fairs, rodeos, and weddings. You name it, he'll go there. He does quite well,

66

and he has a loyal following. And I've always told him he ought to open a restaurant or get a food truck. I'm glad to see it's finally going to happen to him.

I made it inside the airport and saw the line to go through the security checkpoint was starting to back up. I still had plenty of time to get to the gate and get my seat assignment. Even though this airline makes you feel like you're getting a lottery ticket to get your seat number. You still feel like you're going through a cattle chute to get your seat. I went over to the ticket kiosk and got my boarding pass. I'm in the second group. I made it through security and found a seat at the gate and sat down. I glanced over at this guy reading the Spokesman-Review. On the cover was Nina's picture, the headline read, "Local Sports Celebrity Found Murdered." Then it hit me. I'm going to a funeral. I hate funerals. I try to avoid them if I can. Not only do I have a funeral to attend; I got to find out who murdered Nina and all the other golfers. I tried to shut my eyes when I heard the annoying female announcement you hear all over the airport, "Rogers, Mr. Harold Rogers, please pick up a white courtesy phone." I always wondered what that person must look like and is this their only job?

Finally, they announced that our flight was ready to begin general boarding and for us to make our way over to the corresponding chutes.

I was in the second group 31-45. I should still be able to get an aisle seat. I headed towards the back of the plane. Unfortunately, the seats with the most legroom, the emergency exits, were already taken. I hope I will be able to get a little more sleep on the plane. I stowed my backpack in the overhead bin and settled into my seat. There is one thing I enjoy about being Black when I fly on this airline. If the flight is not completely booked, no one will sit by me. It's not that I am ugly or that I look threatening. Wait a minute, maybe I do look threatening. White people will sit in the center seat to avoid sitting next to me. It happens every single time I fly. It's not just me, I see it with other Black people as well. Believe it or not, this isn't just in Spokane, but every single city that this airline flies. This is not Southwest's fault, but an underlying fact that subtle racism is still prevalent today in America. On a day that I would enjoy this opportunity of sitting alone and getting some sleep, a lady and her two children were the last to board. As the flight attendant picked up the handset and paged her counterpart in the rear of the airplane. I could see her pointing in my direction. The male flight attendant came up, tapped me on my shoulder from behind, and asked, "Would you be so kind to offer up your seat so this lady and her children can sit together?"

My first thought was, hell no! I asked him, "Where will I sit?"

"Well, sir, we only have one seat available, and it is a center seat in the back."

At this very moment, everyone was anxious to take off and now it looks like I am keeping us from pulling back away from the gate. The plane is already thirty minutes late, to begin with, and all they need is a longer delay because of me. I said, "Sure." I reluctantly unbuckled my seatbelt and got up. I reached in and grabbed my backpack from the overhead bin. I saw from the nametag that I was following Mark, the flight attendant, to my new seat.

Mark looked at me and told me, "I appreciate you doing this, I will make it up to you."

"You better," I said.

Mark smiled at me and walked away. I didn't like the way he smiled back at me though. It looked like he may have an ulterior motive. I unlatched the overhead bin, and it was already stuffed with luggage, boxes, and computer bags. And, to make matters worse; besides me sitting in the center seat; I am sandwiched between two men who need to use extensions with their seatbelts so they can fit. I had to stow my backpack under the seat in front of me. I felt like I was a sardine in a can of mackerel. The lady and her two screaming kids finally settled into their seats.

CHAPTER FOUR

SOUND OF THE WAVES

Unfortunately, I was unable to get any rest on the flight. Mark did keep his word and asked me, "Can I get you something to drink? On the house, of course?"

Even though it was so early in the morning, I was still reeling from my hangover. I thought to myself, if I took a bite from the hair of the dog that bit me, I might feel better. "How about a Bloody Mary?" I asked. Mark came back a few minutes later with my ingredients to make my drink. He gave me a wink and left. Surprisingly enough, the drink did help me feel better. I had to change planes in Portland to make my connecting flight to San Jose. Since we were thirty minutes late leaving Spokane, I had only fifteen minutes to get to make my connection. The gate was at another concourse. I had to run to get there on time. There wasn't an old lady yelling at me shouting, "Go O.J. go!" I was in the last group boarding, which assured me that I would be sitting in a center seat again.

I glanced through the latest issue of Golf Digest and saw problems I need to work on. The magazine covers the whole litany of problems that I share with a million other golfers. For example, Cure Your Slice, Hit the Ball Farther, Sink Those Putts, Hit the Ball Farther, and Which Ball to Use. The list goes on and on. Finally, the fasten your seatbelt light came on and the flight attendant's voice came over the intercom announcing, "We are starting our initial descent into San Jose, please make sure your tray tables are locked back into place and your seatbacks are in their upright position."

I peered out the window and I could see the thick inversion layer welcoming me to San Jose, California. I made the sign of the cross when we landed and waited to hear the chime indicating that we were at the gate, and it was okay for us to get up out of our seats. I was looking forward to seeing Long Ball again, even though it was not under the best of circumstances.

I followed the signs in the terminal directing me over to baggage claim. Once there, I saw other people from my flight going over to Carrousel number four. Then I heard the familiar voice, "Hey Clancy, over here!" Long Ball yelled.

We gave each other a big bear hug. "Good to see you, buddy," I said.

"I thought you missed your flight. I was beginning to wonder when it looked like no one else was coming over to claim their bags."

"Sorry about that, I was the last one off because I sat in the very last row. I hope my bags made it?"

"Did you bring your sticks?"

"Of course, I did."

"Great, do you want to play at Pebble Beach?"

"Are you serious?"

"You bet. We got a 2:30 tee time. We will get down there by 1:00 and we can get a bite to eat before we play."

"Gosh Long Ball, do you know how long I have dreamed of playing at Pebble Beach? Several years ago, I was in Sacramento visiting my brother. I decided to take a drive to Monterey. I took a drive on the famous '17 Mile Drive' and I found myself following signs to Pebble Beach. As I approached the course, I thought of all the history and drama that has taken place at this prestigious landmark golf course. My hands started to sweat with excitement as I walked to the clubhouse. I looked at the names of the past winners on the wall with the likes of Davis Love III, Tiger Woods, and Payne Stewart. I went over to the Number One Tee and stood there in awe," I said.

"The starter came over to me and asked me, "What time are you scheduled to tee off?"

"I'm not playing today," I told him.

"We can fit you in," he said.

"You don't know how bad I want to play. This is like being on hallowed ground," I said.

"It sure is. You can go walk over to Number 17 and walk up 18 if you like," he suggested.

"Are you sure it's, okay?"

"Of course, people do it all the time."

"He pointed out the way for me to go to get over to 17. I couldn't believe how awesome it was to see the infamous Par-3 17th. There was a foursome about to hit. I watched them hit into the wind. Out of the four, one guy made it onto the green. As they were privileged to walk on the fairway, I walked along the cart path. Finally, they came to the Par-5 18th. With the sounds of the waves and the beauty of this hole, I thought of all the past champions who played here. This was such a neat experience. I promised myself that someday I was going to play this course. And now, because of you, Long Ball, it is going to come true. I can't thank you enough."

"Clancy, I just wanted to thank you for your help. I'm glad you made it down here."

"No problem, this will give us some time to talk about the case and plan out the strategy we need to protect you at the Open."

Finally, my golf clubs and luggage made it to the carousel. Long Ball and I went out to the parking lot and to my surprise, this beautiful Maserati Quattroporte started up all by itself.

"Is that your Maserati?" I asked with excitement.

"You bet. How else could I start it?"

I looked around and we were the only people in this section of the parking lot.

"Pretty slick, eh Clancy?"

"You got a remote started on that?"

"Yup."

"When did you get this gorgeous car Long Ball?"

"I got it about two weeks ago. It came with the remote starter and security system as part of the package."

Long Ball closed the trunk after we put my luggage and clubs inside. I couldn't wait to get on the road and see what this baby could do. "I can't get over this car Long Ball. It is unbelievable. What kind of blue do they call this?"

"Why, Blu Nobile Tri-Coat of course. And the interior is Rosso/Nero. Don't you find it charming and exquisite?"

"It is at that. Couldn't Maserati just call it Red and Black for us normal folks? It sounds so Italian."

"That's the Italians for you," Long Ball said.

It's amazing what money can get you, I thought to myself. Not only do you have these plush leather seats that mold to your body, there is a High Gloss Piano with Black Trim, plus a magnificent sound system. "What else does this car have Long Ball?"

"Check this out, Clancy. I got this GPS which tells me where I want to go, and it will give me a turn-by-turn route to take. It comes on to warn me if I make a wrong turn and recalculates my route. It is so much better than the one that comes with your cell phone. The bigger screen works wonders. I don't have to strain my eyes to see the screen like the one on my phone."

"Sorry Long Ball, but that information has been out for a long time. You're still old-school, aren't you?'

"Yes, I am. I used to call Nina, my IT Director because she would help me out with all these fancy gadgets and stuff."

"Did you enter the information for Pebble Beach?"

"Don't worry Clancy, I got everything set. Just sit back and relax."

"How long will it take us to get there LB?"

"About an hour and a half. It's a nice drive and we can get a chance to talk."

"How's your brother doing?"

"He's taking it pretty hard; we all are."

"Have the police found anything?"

"Not yet Clancy, that's why I want you here. I need your help."

"Sure, no problem. I will do my best."

We finally made it to the entrance of the famous 17-Mile Drive. My hands were sweating with every turn knowing that I was getting closer to my dream, and it was about to come true. The view of the ocean is truly spectacular with its vibrant blue-green colors. It was breathtaking to be this close to the water again and see the surf crash onto the beach. There were people riding bikes, and jogging along the path, while others were walking their dogs. All of them enjoying this private little playground.

"Clancy, we have plenty of time. Let's pull over and eat our lunch."

"Are you sure we have enough time to do this?" I asked.

"Clancy, I'm just as excited to play as you are. Let's take ten minutes to eat and enjoy this view."

"Okay."

Long Ball pulled into a parking area where there were a few picnic tables right off the beach. As soon as we got out of the car, I could smell the salty air and feel the wind blowing against me. The air was cooler than it was at the San Jose Airport.

"Long Ball, could you pop the trunk? I need to get my windbreaker."

Long Ball grabbed a small cooler out of the trunk and handed me my windbreaker. I pulled it over my bald head and felt some relief from the cool breeze. We walked down some sandy steps

76

over to where the picnic tables were and sat down. I was trying to soak in all the splendor of the rhythm of the waves crashing against the rocks, the greenish blue water, and the beautiful cloudless sky. There were pieces of driftwood scattered across other parts of the beach. You could see a group of seagulls perched on the rock outcroppings as if they were guarding their sanctuary. A lone pelican dove into the water and came out with his beak wrapped around the catch of the day. And farther off was a huge rock that had hundreds of sea lions camped out enjoying the sun.

"We sure picked a great day to play, eh Clancy?"

Long Ball opened the cooler and handed me a white box lunch and a soda.

"Here you go Clancy. They are both turkey on rye, Swiss cheese, horseradish, mayo, lettuce with no tomato."

"Hey Long Ball, you remembered."

"I know how much you dislike tomatoes."

I opened the box, took out my sandwich and grabbed the jalapeno potato chips. Underneath that was a chocolate chip cookie for dessert.

"Boy Long Ball you thought of everything. The only thing that's missing is a shot of Jack."

Long Ball reached inside the cooler and pulled out a flask and two shot glasses. He didn't even give me a chance to say no and just filled up the glasses.

"To Nina," he said.

"To Nina," I replied as our glasses met.

I started to sip it and said to Long Ball, "What the hell," and slammed it down.

There was a moment of silence. It wasn't planned, it just happened. I looked over at Long Ball and his eyes were welling up like mine. I took a bite of my sandwich and felt a shockwave go to my sinuses and to the back of my head from the horseradish. Long Ball started to laugh.

"I had the deli put extra horseradish on yours. I know how much you like it."

"That's pretty good," I said.

"Did you want another shot Clancy?"

"No, I better not. I want to try to play halfway decent today."

I grabbed the empty boxes and put the sandwich wrappers inside and the empty potato chip bags as well. We both got up from the picnic table and tossed our trash into the garbage can. We climbed back up the sandy steps to the parking lot. Long Ball pushed a button on his key fob and started the car. He hit another button which opened the trunk and he put the cooler back inside. I took one last look at the beach as we pulled out of the parking lot.

"Thanks for stopping here," I said.

"No problem, Clancy."

Every turn along the road had a new surprise; either it was a breathtaking view of the ocean, Cypress Trees, or magnificent homes.

"Long Ball, how do these people afford these homes?"

"Old money and people that made it through the dot com crash," he said.

"I'm sure of that. These views are unbelievable."

"Wait until you see some of the views from the golf course."

"Long Ball, how was it when you first played Pebble?"

"Probably just how you feel right now; all knotted up and nervous inside. You don't know what to expect. But look on the bright side Clancy; you're not in a tournament like I was. You only have to put up with me today. Not thousands of spectators."

Long Ball turned into the entrance of Pebble Beach. There it was before me, in its magnificent splendor. I wanted to soak up every little detail about this place. My dream is about to come true.

A valet came over to us.

"Can I take your golf clubs?"

He immediately recognized Long Ball.

"How are you doing Mr. Jackson? We've been expecting you and your guest to show up," he said.

Long Ball reached into his left pocket, pulled out his money clip and gave the valet ten dollars.

"Long Ball are you nuts?" I asked.

"Clancy, one thing about Pebble, it's expensive. Get used to it."

"It's a little bit warmer here than it was at the beach. Long Ball, I think I'll leave my jacket."

"I wouldn't do that if I were you Clancy. You may want to bring your sweater and rain gear just in case. You just don't know how these weather conditions can change so quickly."

We walked towards the clubhouse which is over by the putting green. There is a large plaque on the wall with the names of past champions: Tiger Woods, Jack Nicholas, Tom Watson, Phil Mickelson, Payne Stewart, Johnny Miller, and others.

"Long Ball, it's a who's who of golf."

We walked inside the pro shop, and everyone shouted, "Hey Long Ball!"

"This is just like Cheers Long Ball," I said.

"Gene, I like you to meet a really good friend of mine, Harry Clancy."

"Harry, how are you doing?" Gene asked.

"Just great, please, call me Clancy. All my friends do."

"Fair enough Clancy. Is this your first time playing at Pebble Beach?"

"Yes, it is, and I am so excited to play here."

"We'll make sure you have an enjoyable round. You're not set to tee off for a few more minutes," Gene said.

'What do you want to do Clancy?" asked Long Ball.

"I feel like I need to go run a couple of miles to settle down. I'm so keyed up."

"Let's stretch and go hit a bucket of balls and loosen up a bit Clancy."

"Sounds like a good idea."

The valet brought our clubs over to the pro shop.

We got into our golf cart and made it over to the driving range.

I grabbed my 8-iron, pitching wedge, and 5-wood to loosen up with. Long Ball grabbed his 8-iron, 3-iron, and driver. At the driving range, a couple of people came up to Long Ball and asked him for his autograph. They took a double take at me and realized I wasn't anyone special.

I put my 8-iron behind my neck and started to twist, bend, and stretch to see if I could make these sore muscles work like they were supposed to function. I went over to a vacant spot on the driving range and grabbed a couple of golf balls that were already there waiting for us to use. I took a couple of practice swings first.

"Let's see how it works with a golf ball," I said to Long Ball. I could hear Long Ball already

81

hitting the sweet spot with his 8-iron. I brought the club back low and slow. I made good solid contact, and the ball went 150 years. I started to hit one ball after another. Then I heard Long Ball.

"Still hitting like you're a machine gun, eh Clancy? What did I tell you?"

"Slow down and take your time when you're on the range."

We hit a few more balls and drove back to the clubhouse and put our clubs back in our golf bags. We grabbed our putters and went over to the putting green.

The starter's voice came over the intercom and said, "Next on the number one tee, the McDonald party, followed by the Jackson twosome and the Jones twosome on deck."

"How do you feel Clancy?"

"I feel pretty good. I dropped a few good four-footers on the practice green. I just wonder how I will do on the real deal."

"Don't worry, you'll do okay. We better go and check in with the starter."

"Here we are Clancy. What do you think? Pretty impressive, isn't it? You're standing on the number one tee at Pebble Beach."

"Long Ball, it's unbelievable."

The starter's voice came over the intercom again and announced, "Next on the number one tee, the Jackson twosome and the Jones twosome."

Our caddies came over and introduced themselves. "Welcome to Pebble Beach, I'm Johnny O'Brien and this is Tom Dempsey. Have you played here before Mr. Clancy? I've seen you play here before Mr. Jackson, welcome back."

"No Johnny, this is my first time," I said.

"How long have you been a caddie at Pebble Beach?" I asked.

Johnny looked at me with a wide grin and said, "Almost twenty years."

"Great, you'll be my caddy," I said.

"Mr. Clancy, we already decided who we were going to be with when we saw you in the pro shop." Johnny said.

"How about you Tom, how long have you been here?" I asked.

"I'm the new guy. Just twelve years," he said.

The starter came over and introduced us to Marcus and Rodney Jones. "Enjoy your round gentlemen."

The four of us looked at each other and started laughing.

"What are the odds that we would get paired up with another Black twosome?" I asked.

"Did they do this on purpose?" I asked.

Marcus replied, "Don't play the race card yet."

We all laughed. Long Ball took a golf tee and flipped it into the air. Whomever it pointed to after it landed went first until everyone in the group had a spot.

Fortunately, Long Ball was first, Marcus, Rodney, and me. I'm batting cleanup.

It took me a couple of holes to get my nerves to settle down. All the excitement of playing at Pebble Beach made me nervous and anxious. I got back-to-back triple bogeys on the first two holes. Long Ball on the other hand, birdied number one and just missed another birdie on two.

He told me, "Clancy, you need to settle down and not let the course intimidate you."

"I suppose you're right."

"Pretend you're playing the Creek at Qualchan, and you just ripped your drive 255 yards on number three past the big evergreen tree in the middle of the fairway. You're still 280 yards out. You're getting your rhythm together now. Your swing feels good. Take your 7-iron and lay up so you'll be a wedge away. Wouldn't it make sense to be 120 yards out instead of using your 3-wood and be in the water? Play smart."

"Course management," I said.

"Exactly," he said.

Rodney and Marcus were doing okay. It turns out that Rodney owns a Lexus dealership in Seaside, which is just outside of Monterey. His son Marcus is the General Manager of the dealership, so they get to play Pebble Beach and Spyglass a lot. They know the course quite well.

The caddies were full of information and supplied us with plenty of stories.

Our group was walking up to the ninth hole, which is a 460-yard Par-4. The last guy in the group in front of us just hit a nice shot; about 245 yards.

Johnny said, "That's a great shot. You don't want to overdo it on this hole. Making a par on this hole is like making a birdie. This is the hardest hole on the course. Hit your 3-wood. There is a fairway bunker on the left and three more to deal with on the left side as well. And don't forget the big Pacific Ocean on your right."

I looked over at Johnny and said, "Thanks for the wonderful words of encouragement."

He smiled and said, "No problem."

"Johnny, how did you decided to become a caddy?" I asked.

"Would you believe I was a stockbroker in New York?"

"Get out of here! Are you serious?"

"Really, I was. My wife and I came out here on vacation and we just fell in love with this place. We were tired of the rat race in New York. While I was playing, my mind started to give me images of my life before me. It was kind of surreal like. My view of my life showed me what I gave up. All I wanted was to be a top performer for the company. I neglected my family. My children were growing up and without knowing their father. After being here for a few days, I started to relax, and I slowed down. A calmness, or peace if you will, came over me and I liked it."

I took his advice and hit my 3-wood 245 yards right down the middle of the fairway.

"Good shot Clancy," Johnny said to me as he took my club and put it back into my golf bag.

"Tell me more about you moving out here."

"Sure, no problem, we were only supposed to be here for a week. The first few days I was calling the office to check in. My wife was getting upset. She kept reminding me we were on vacation. Finally, on the third day, my wife had enough. She gave me an ultimatum. If you call the office today, I'm leaving you."

"Get out of here. She really threatened you like that?" I asked in disbelief.

"She sure did. I've been married long enough to know when I press the wrong buttons that she will get upset. You're about 217 yards out. I would recommend a 4-iron or 5-wood sir."

I looked over and saw Rodney hit out of a fairway bunker. Marcus hit a great shot with his 3-iron and landed on the green. "Johnny, I'll take my 5-wood."

I took an easy swing and landed on the fringe of the green leaving me with a 30-footer.

"Good job Mr. Clancy," Jonny said.

As we got closer to the green, I saw that Long Ball was about four feet away from getting a birdie. "So, Johnny what happened?"

"My wife and I had a come-to-Jesus meeting that night at a nice Italian place overlooking the water in Monterey, Little Luigi's. Our lives changed that night. We just started talking about our priorities and our lifestyle. We knew we needed a change. This just didn't happen overnight. I was all stressed out from work, and I was bringing it home. You can tell when things aren't going right when your family isn't all that thrilled when you come home. And the first thing I did was to have a drink the minute I walked in the door."

We were still waiting for Rodney to make it onto the green. He topped the ball on his third shot, and it only went about forty yards. Finally, he got on the green.

"If I can two-putt this I'll be happy Johnny."

I was away so I putted first. I hit it too hard, and it rolled past the hole by seven feet. Everyone else got close but no one got inside Long Ball's four-footer. Since I was still away, it was my turn to putt. The ball went in. I raised my hands up in the air. "That was my best putt of the day!" I shouted.

"Nice putt," everyone said as I reached in the cup to grab my ball.

Long Ball naturally made his birdie. Rodney got a double bogey while Marcus squeezed out a bogey. We started to drive over to the next hole. I asked Johnny more questions about his move to California. "What did the children think about the move when you told them?"

"Well, that night over dinner, we made the decision if we wanted to save our marriage and keep our children happy, we need to do something different. Of course, when we told the kids, they flipped out. What about our friends? Where are we going to go to school? The next morning when we woke up it was like a weight had been lifted off our shoulders. We made the decision to move to California. I told my wife that I was going to see if I could get on here as a caddie. As we talked over breakfast that morning, we looked at the numbers. I had saved enough money from our investments plus the sale of our house we could survive quite well. My wife also mentioned that maybe she could revive the catering business she used to run before we got married. And, as they say, the rest is history. It's been a really great move for us. The kids are happy. My wife is doing quite well and I'm working at one of the most beautiful places in the world. Who could ask for anything better?"

"That's wonderful Johnny. Not too many people get to do what you and your family have done. That's amazing."

"You're right Mr. Clancy. What type of work do you do?"

"I'm a private investigator."

"Really, kind of like Magnum P.I.?"

"Well sort of, except I don't solve my cases in sixty-minutes."

"What brings you out here? Are you working on a case?"

"Yes, I am as a matter of fact. Long Ball's niece was murdered a few days ago.

"Are you talking about Nina Jackson from Stanford?"

"Yes."

"My daughter is on the golf team with her. They were really good friends."

"My god, you're kidding me, I need to talk to her."

"What are you doing for dinner tonight?" Johnny asked.

"Johnny, what's that got to do with me meeting your daughter?"

"Everything, she works in Carmel at Clint Eastwood's old restaurant, The Hog's Breath Inn."

"You can set it up?"

Johnny reached into his pocket and pulled out his cell phone and called his daughter.

"It's all set. We have dinner reservations at eight. The reservations are under my name."

"What do you mean under your name?"

As soon as I asked that, Long Ball said, "Guess who's coming to dinner?"

"Did you all just set me up?"

"Sure did," Long Ball grinned. I've known Johnny for a long time. We met each other at one of the girls' tournaments. We have been friends ever since. Also, we will be spending the night at their place tonight. Remember that big spread we saw on the way here?"

"Don't tell me that's Johnny's?"

I looked over at Johnny and now he's the one with the big grin on his face. I glanced over at Rodney and Marcus.

"Don't look at us, I know nothing." Marcus said.

"Me neither," chimed Rodney as he laughed.

I settled down and got into a nice groove for the rest of the back nine. As we approached number 17, one of the most spectacular Par-3's in the world, I felt really blessed to be here. It's too bad that somebody got murdered that brings me here. But I am savoring the moment.

The shadows were getting longer as the sun was going into its final descent for the day. We will have just enough light to finish. I was 8 over and I wanted to see if I could break 80. I would be happy with 80. However, if I could tell the boys back home that I got a 79 at Pebble Beach that would be awesome. Long Ball was the first to hit. Since we're playing from the blues, 17 is playing 178 yards. Just past the tee box on the right stands several Italian Spruce trees at attention as if they were going to block the wind for you. It's not the wind from the side you're concerned about, but the wind that's blowing into your face from the ocean. You have this magnificent backdrop of the ocean behind the green. If the wind isn't enough to contend with, don't forget the six bunkers surrounding the green: especially the big one on the left. I was surprised to see that Long Ball's caddie gave him his 5-iron when he asked for his 6-iron.

"With this stiff wind, you need a longer club, please take it," his caddie pleaded.

"If I sail it over the green there will be no tip for you," said Long Ball.

"So, you'll double it if you land on the green within ten feet of the pin Mr. Jackson if it's the right club?" his caddie asked.

"Absolutely, better yet, I will triple it." Long Ball said.

We all stopped to watch this event unfold. Not only was Long Ball determined to make this shot, but he also stood over the ball a little longer than normal. But when he let loose on the ball with his 5-iron it sailed straight as an arrow within five feet of the pin. That caddie was all smiles because he just made $150. You could tell he wanted to say I told you so, but he held back. Long Ball on the other hand was ecstatic with his shot.

"Son, that was worth the money. Let me tell you something, I was going to be all over your behind if that ball did not make it to the green," said Long Ball as he gave him his 5-iron to put back into his golf bag. His caddie kept smiling at Long Ball.

"Wipe that stupid grin off your face," Long Ball said.

At that remark, everyone started busting up laughing. "Make sure he gives you cash," I said. I took my 4-iron and launched it. My ball landed just shy of the green. I would really have to scramble to make par. Marcus and Rodney both missed the green as well. Marcus landed in the greenside bunker on the left and Rodney was right off the green although pin high. He would have to pitch over the bunker, which always adds a little more pressure on the shot.

"Clancy, do a bump and run with your 8-iron," Johnny told me as he handed me my club.

"You're the boss," I told him.

"You're forty feet away Clancy, make sure you don't hit it too hard and roll it off the green. You want to land about twenty feet, and have it roll within five feet or closer," he said.

"That sounds good to me," I said. It was a perfect shot, and it came within two feet of the hole, just inside Long Ball's shot. Rodney tried to pitch over the bunker and caught the lip and it trickled back down into the bunker. It took Rodney two shots to get out and he finished with a double bogey. Marcus hit a fantastic shot and got a sand save to end up with a par. And of course, Long Ball got his birdie. I made my two-footer to get a par.

As we were coming up to the 18th, I started thinking how realistic it would be for me to birdie 18 and finish with a 79. Number 18 is a 543-yard par-5 and the third hardest hole on the course. I've seen this hole so many times on TV that I know it by heart. I always tried to imagine what it would be like standing on the tee at 18 knowing that I needed a birdie to win the championship. However, seeing it up close and personal is completely different. Here is this picturesque hole where so many championships have been won or lost. And here I am, playing one of the most magnificent holes on the planet.

Long Ball was first up with his birdie on 17. True to form, Long Ball crushed his ball 260 yards going left to right hugging the dogleg left along the ocean that left him in perfect position. Marcus was up next. His shot never made it to the safety of the fairway. His ball hooked and landed on the rocks below before it bounced into the ocean to its watery grave. Marcus decided to hit another ball from the tee, and it landed about 220 yards on the right side of the fairway, and he breathed a sigh of relief.

Just as I started to address the ball, I pictured Payne Stewart's swing he made when he won the championship. I made one of the best drives in my entire life, straight down the middle ten yards past Long Ball's.

"Nice drive Clancy," Long Ball said as he patted me on my back.

"Thank you, coach, yours wasn't too bad either," I said in return.

After a couple of worm burners, Marcus, and Rodney both struggled to get down the fairway by hitting the famous Cyprus tree. Long Ball took his 3-wood and landed on the green in two, still sixty feet away. I don't know what got into me. I tried to do the same thing. Unfortunately, I caught a branch from the Cyprus tree and landed forty yards out. I took my sand wedge and pulled it left. I landed in the sand trap. I was lying three and still had a chance to make par. My chances of making birdie just died right before me as Marcus yelled, "Beach!"

As I approached the sand trap, I had a great lie. If I can get the ball close enough, I can at least save par. I grounded my feet real solid in the sand and made a perfect swing as the ball flew out perfectly. I couldn't see the hole from where I was standing. I ran out just in time to see my ball hit the pin and drop in for a birdie. I raised my hands just like the pros as if I won the AT&T Tournament.

Long Ball still had his putt for birdie and of course, he made it. He was so happy for me. I took off my hat and shook hands with everyone.

"Excellent job Clancy, that was a great shot," Long Ball said as he shook my hand and patted me on the back again.

CHAPTER FIVE

A SURPRISED LOOK

"I cannot believe I birdied 18 at Pebble Beach," I said to Long Ball as I met him in the lobby of the men's locker room. You know that was the most invigorating shower I have ever experienced too. Long Ball laughed.

We decided we would meet Johnny and his wife at the Hog's Breath Inn instead of stopping at his place. Johnny had some work to finish up before he could leave. As we were driving towards Carmel-By-The-Sea, Long Ball reminded me why we were down here in the first place. "I hope Johnny's daughter will be able to give us something to go on," he said.

His remark popped my bubble, "I hope so as well," I said.

A black S500 Mercedes was coming down the driveway of the house that Long Ball was pointing at and said, "Hey Clancy, there's Johnny's house, looks like our timing is perfect." Johnny honked the horn as we sped by them. His wife waved at us to let us know that they saw us.

There were a lot of people strolling up and down the sidewalk going in and out of the many boutiques as we entered town. We found a place to park a couple of blocks from the restaurant. It felt good to get out and walk. I felt a little stiff from playing today and from the plane ride.

"I'm running on adrenaline Long Ball," I said. We walked inside the restaurant and stepped up to the hostess station. Just below the hostess station was an oval sign, which read, Welcome to The Hog's Breath Inn. A wooden cabinet with glass doors was next to it which had on display an assortment of Hog's Breath merchandise; shirts, mugs, tee shirts, hats, sweatshirts, and shot glasses that tourists were so eager to buy.

"Welcome to Hog's Breath Inn. Do you have a reservation?" the hostess asked.

"Yes, we do Elaine," Long Ball replied after reading her nametag. "It's under O'Brien."

"Great, we've been expecting you," Elaine said.

At that moment, this beautiful petite Irish redhead came around the corner screaming, "Hey Uncle Long Ball!" as she gave him a big hug.

"Hey there Sarah, how are you doing sweetie? You look beautiful as ever. How are you hitting?" asked Long Ball.

"Not bad, I finished number two, right behind Nina this season."

As soon as Sarah said Nina's name, she started crying.

Long Ball put his arm around her to console her as she looked up at him and said, "I'm sorry Uncle Long Ball."

"That's okay sweetie, I understand. I miss her too."

At that moment Sarah's parents walked in. "Hey Sarah, what's wrong sweetheart?" Johnny asked with a concerned look on his face.

"I'm sorry daddy. I mentioned Nina's name and I just lost it."

"Are you okay?" her mother asked.

"I'll be fine momma."

Her mother looked over at me and extended her hand to introduce herself to me. "I'm Maria O'Brien, you must be Harry Clancy. I've heard all about you from Long Ball," she said still holding onto my hand.

"Yes, I am Mrs. O'Brien. It is a pleasure to meet you."

"What's bothering you, Mr. Clancy?" Mrs. O'Brien asked as she finally let go of my hand.

"Mr. Clancy, I must warn you, my wife is very perceptive and can tell a lot about someone by their hands," explained Johnny.

"Something is bothering you Mr. Clancy. Something about your past, isn't it?" she asked.

"Yes, how perceptive of you Mrs. O'Brien," I replied. Fortunately, she doesn't know that my uneasiness stems from me seeing

Tanya again, the woman that I was supposed to marry.

"She's a beautiful woman. You must let go of the pain and hurt that she caused you so you can move on," Maria said.

"Stop that!" I said. "Long Ball, did you tell her anything about Tanya?"

"I never told her anything about Tanya," Long Ball said.

"Mom, dad, I have your favorite table outside all ready for you guys, please follow me," Sarah said.

We walked through the restaurant passing several stone fireplaces and an array of Western motif objects decorating the walls. Most interesting were the two hogs' heads: with a stunned look on their faces. One was over the fireplace. The other was on the adjacent wall next to a yoke that would have been used with horses or oxen years ago at a different time. The oil lanterns glowing from atop the burl wood tables were casting shadows on the napkins, which appeared to be standing at attention. As we got closer to the outside, we still had to make our way through the bar. The wooden bar was small with a couple of patrons laughing as they drank pints of their favorite ale. An open leaded glass window overlooked the patio. There was a door that led to the outside. Finally, we made it outside to our table. The brick patio matched the three brick and stone fireplaces that surrounded the

98

patio. The burl wood tables with the iron and wood slats were like the same chairs that matched the motif inside.

Sarah motioned the waitress to come over to our table to take our drink orders. Long Ball and I opted for Guinness while Maria and Johnny ordered a Chardonnay. Sarah excused herself to go help the waitress with our drink orders.

"Mrs. O'Brien, how were you able to see so much about me from my hands?" I asked.

"Mr. Clancy, it is a gift I inherited from my mother when I was a little girl," she said.

"Please call me Clancy," I told her.

"Okay, Clancy. My mother always told me I was special. I had no idea how painful it would be for me. When we were living in New York, I helped the police with several high-profile cases," she explained.

"That's absolutely amazing. How could you tell that I was upset?" I asked.

"Clancy, it's not that you are upset," Maria said as she grabbed my hands again. "You are confused about having to face something from your past that is disturbing you. Tell me about this woman."

"Tanya and I were supposed to get married. We had a great relationship, so I thought. We bought a house together and we were looking forward to starting our life together. But on our wedding day, she decided not to show up. She jilted me."

"That must have been very painful for you Mr. Clancy."

"What must have been painful?" Sarah asked as she placed our drinks on the table.

"I was just telling your mother about me being jilted at the altar."

"I see my mother has got her death grip on you. Be very careful, she has tendency to pry into your business."

"Okay," I said as I withdrew my hands from Mrs. O'Brien.

"Sarah, don't talk about your mother like that!" Johnny said with a stern look on his face.

"I'm sorry daddy."

"It's not me you should be apologizing to?"

"I'm sorry momma, Uncle Long Ball and Mr. Clancy," Sarah said with her voice trembling.

Mrs. O'Brien looked at her daughter with tears in her eyes and said, "That's okay honey, I forgive you."

I looked at Long Ball to see if he had that same shocked reaction I had to Sarah's comment. He looked just as surprised as me. Our waitress came by with our menus and told us that, "My name is Sally, and I will be serving you this evening. The special is blackened salmon, asparagus with hollandaise sauce, roasted red potatoes and a Caesar Salad."

"It is Daddy's favorite!" Sarah blurted out.

100

"I'll be back in a few minutes. Can I get you anything else?" the waitress asked.

"Could you bring us some water, and could I have some lemon in mine please?" I asked.

Long Ball looked over at me and was laughing. "You picked up that lemon thing from Tanya, didn't you?"

"Yes, I did," I said.

As Maria got up to excuse herself to go to the ladies' room she said, "Mr. Clancy, you must tell me more about this woman."

She motioned to her daughter and told her, "Please come with me." The two women got up and left together with her mother holding onto her daughter's arm with a tight grip.

Johnny looked over at both of us and apologized for his daughter's outburst. "I'm sorry you had to see that. Generally, Sarah's has always been even keeled. Ever since Nina's death, she hasn't been the same."

"I can understand Johnny, how was their relationship?" I asked.

"Clancy, they were the best of friends, both on and off the course," Johnny said. "What are you getting at Mr. Clancy?"

"Johnny, please forgive my friend, he didn't mean any harm," said Long Ball.

"I'm sorry Johnny; I need to find out everything I can about this case. And I do have to ask questions. I wasn't implying anything about your daughter," I said.

However, your response is quite interesting, I said to myself. I wonder what else he may be hiding.

"Did I miss anything?" Maria asked, excluding her daughter as they sat down.

You could tell that Sarah had been crying. Long Ball gave me a look that I should not say anything. I took his lead and picked up my menu. I really didn't care what I was going to eat right now. I was more interested in what was going on here.

The waitress came over and asked us, "Are you ready to order now?"

I was going to tell her to give us another five minutes, but Mrs. O'Brien didn't give me a chance. She told the waitress, "Please bring us three of the specials." Jonny just shook his head in agreement.

"What will you have sir?" she asked looking over at Long Ball.

"I'll have the Dirty Harry Dinner," Long Ball said.

"And you sir?"

I took a quick glance at the menu to see what was included with the Dirty Harry Dinner. Hmm, chopped sirloin, wild mushrooms, horseradish, and a wholegrain mustard sauce with garlic mashed potatoes. "I'll have the Dirty Harry Burger and the Hog's Breath Baby Back Ribs."

"How do you want your burger sir?"

"Medium works for me."

"How are you all doing on your drinks? Can I bring you another round?"

Before we could say anything, Sarah said, "A shot of tequila and a Corona back and another round for everyone else."

We all shook our heads in agreement. Mother like daughter I said to myself.

With that, Sally walked off but turned around like Colombo to ask another question. "You are off work, aren't you Sarah?" Sally asked.

"Yes, I am," she said.

"Sarah, how long have you two been roommates?" I asked.

"We met our freshman year when we both turned out for the golf team."

"How soon was it before you became roommates?"

"I was going to get to that as soon as you give me a chance to answer."

"My bad," I said.

"It was our sophomore year. Our relationship started off a little rocky at first."

"How was that?" I asked.

"Well, everyone on the team had a hard time adjusting to Nina. She was the first Black woman golfer on the team, and she was so damn good."

"Were you jealous?"

"Who wouldn't be? She was gorgeous and talented, and she was winning. Nina made us all look bad. It was really hard for us to get to her level. Nina was so good; she was even beating the seniors on the team. The coach loved her."

"Who's your coach?" I asked as I pulled out my phone to take some notes.

"Here name is Patty Hill. What are you doing Mr. Clancy?" Sarah asked with a concerned look on her face.

"I'm putting her name into my phone for future reference," I said.

"Sarah, Mr. Clancy is a private investigator and I hired him to find out who killed Nina, as well as to protect me," explained Long Ball.

"Why would you need protection Uncle Long Ball? Who would want to hurt you?" Sarah asked.

"That's a good question I'd like to find out myself. I haven't done anything wrong except win a few tournaments," said Long Ball.

"I don't know if you know this or not, but there is a serial killer out there who is murdering Black golfers. You don't suppose the killer is jealous do you Sarah?" I asked.

"But Uncle Long Ball, I don't consider you Black. You're not like them," Sarah said ignoring my question.

I felt a kick on my shin from underneath the table. Long Ball looked up at me with the same shocked look on his face but not as dramatic as

104

mine. I knew Long Ball must have thought my eyeballs were going to pop out of my head from my reaction to Sarah's comment.

"Well, sweetie, I'll take that as a compliment I guess?" Now it was my turn to kick Long Ball in the shins. He looked over at me and smiled. "No matter what you think, I am Black and there are people out there that do not like us. It is a cruel world, but that is reality," he said.

"Well, it's not fair," said Sarah.

My god, is this girl that naïve? I asked myself.

"Could you please excuse me? I'm a little bit chilly." Sarah said as she rose up from the table. "I'm going out to my car to get my sweater," she said.

I watched her walk up the stairs from the patio, which led up to the street. She pulled out her cell phone from her purse once she got to the top of the stairs and started dialing. I got up from my chair and said, "It's my turn to go to the little boy's room. I'll be right back."

I went through the bar and into the main dining room making my way to the hostess stand. "Could you please tell me where the men's room is located?" I asked Elaine, who is still guarding the front door. She pointed me in the right direction. I didn't want to tell her that I saw the sign for the restroom on my way here. What I really wanted to do was check on Sarah. I watched her through the window just around the corner from the hostess stand as she grabbed her sweater from her car and put it on. She was still talking on the cell phone and puffing away on a cigarette making her way back over to the stairs. Sarah had a pained look on her face and seemed to be arguing with the person on the phone.

I did have to relieve myself and went inside the men's room. When I came out of the men's room, I bumped right into Sarah coming out from the bathroom, which was right next door. She reached down to pick up the contents of her purse that fell out when I bumped into her. Sarah was startled when she looked up and saw that it was me that she ran into.

"Oh brother, not you," she said.

"Are you okay?" I asked as I bent down to help her retrieve some of her items that fell out of her purse. I handed over a couple of condoms and her lipstick, which she quickly snatched from my hand.

"I'm okay," she said as she shoved the contents back into her purse.

I couldn't help but notice what appeared to be a blue metal object that is normally associated with a gun barrel. I acted as if I didn't see it and Sarah was none the wiser. "Let's go back outside and join the others," I said helping her up.

"I can manage," she said as she brushed my hand away from her.

Everyone had a surprise look on their faces as we came out from the bar to join them.

"What have you two been up to?" asked Johnny.

"We had a little run in so to speak coming out of the restroom," I said. Sally and another waiter were both carrying out food trays with our dinner as well as our drinks.

"This looks great," I said.

We had a few minutes of silence while everyone was devouring their food. I was just about to take another bite from my hamburger when I looked over and saw this guy coming towards our table. No, it couldn't be, I said to myself.

"Hey Long Ball, how are you doing?" the gentleman asked as he approached our table and shook Long Ball's hand.

"I'm doing pretty good Clint, how about you?" Long Ball asked as he stood up still holding onto Clint's hand. Hey Clint, I would like you to meet a friend of mine. Harry Clancy, this is Mr. Clint Eastwood," he said.

"My god, it's really you. It's a pleasure to meet you Mr. Eastwood," I said as I stood up and extended my hand to shake his.

"And of course, you know the O'Brien's," said Long Ball.

"Johnny, Maria, and Sarah, it's good to see you all again. Long Ball, I'm sorry to hear about your niece," Clint said.

"Thanks, man, I appreciate that," said Long Ball.

107

"What brings you down this way Long Ball?" Clint asked.

"I picked up Harry from the airport this morning. We came down here and played Pebble Beach this afternoon," Long Ball explained.

"Did you caddy for them Johnny?" Clint asked, putting his hand on Johnny's shoulder.

"I certainly did," Johnny said.

"How did you like playing Pebble Beach Mr. Clancy?" asked Clint.

"Please call me Clancy, all my friends do. Pebble Beach was incredible. It was better than I expected; absolutely breathtaking," I said.

"How'd you shoot?" asked Clint.

"I broke eighty and shot a seventy-nine," I said proudly.

"That's fantastic. So, you never played Pebble before?" Clint asked.

"No, never have. This was my first time," I said.

"Long Ball, you better watch it, he may give you a run for your money on the tour," said Clint.

"Where did you fly in from Clancy? Are you from California?" Clint asked.

"No, I'm from Washington State, Spokane actually. I'm down here to attend Nina's funeral and investigate her murder," I said.

"Investigate, are you a cop?"

"No, I'm a private investigator. I used to be a cop," I said divulging more information than I should.

"They don't call you Dirty Harry do they Mr. Clancy?" he asked.

"Every once-in-awhile some idiot will call me that. Oh, I'm sorry, I didn't mean you sir. I am honored that I am with the original Dirty Harry," I said.

"None taken, I get it all the time. Well folks, I have to get going. It was very nice to see you again, Long Ball. Good luck at the Open. And it was a pleasure to meet you Clancy," he said.

"Long Ball, I can't take you anywhere. Do you know everybody on the planet?" I asked, still excited about meeting my favorite actor of all time.

"Just about, I have few billion left still to meet," Long Ball said laughing.

"Clancy, how do you feel about seeing Tanya again?" Maria asked as Sally came back around with the dessert tray and tempted us with something decadent for us to choose.

Not sure what to say I just said, "I'll have to wait and see."

"You won't have to wait very long to see her," Long Ball said.

"I know, I'll probably see her at the funeral," I said.

"Not exactly Clancy," Long Ball said with a smirk on his face.

"What are you up to Long Ball?" I asked with a very concerned look on my face.

"Guess who's coming to dinner tomorrow night at my brother's house?"

"Long Ball you didn't?" I asked.

Sally was still holding the dessert tray in front of us, waiting to hear what our selection was going to be. All of us in unison waived her off. "Is there anything else I can bring you?" Sally asked as she parted with the tray.

"No," I said.

"Clancy let me ask you the question again. How do you feel about seeing Tanya?" Maria asked.

"This puts a different twist on the situation. I wasn't expecting to see her this soon. Not tomorrow anyway," I said.

Maria grabbed my hands again and told me, "Don't worry. I can see that you are quite nervous. Don't be, all of your questions you've held onto over the past twenty years will be answered. Not necessarily tomorrow, but as the walls of resentment, bitterness and anger come down so will the revelation come forth."

"Who are you?" I asked, pulling my hands away from her.

"There's something else I neglected to tell you Clancy. Maria is a clinical psychologist. So, occasionally, or basically all the time, she will

110

psychoanalyze you. You're not safe around her," Johnny said.

"How do you mean?" I asked. "Are you still practicing? I thought you had a catering business?"

"If you haven't noticed it already, my mother is always on me about something and she is always telling me what to do," Sarah said.

"Sweetie, it's just that your father and I want what's best for you. And yes Mr. Clancy, I do have a catering business. I gave up my practice when we moved here. Besides, I do enjoy my catering business and it has been quite profitable for us," Maria said.

"Oh Mother, why don't you just stop with the psychobabble crap!" Sarah shouted as she got up to leave.

Before anyone could say goodbye, Sarah ran up the patio stairs to the parking lot across the street to her car.

"Mr. Clancy and Long Ball, please accept my apologies for my daughter's outburst. I guess Nina's murder has affected her more than I expected," said Johnny.

"That's okay Johnny, I understand," said Long Ball.

"Johnny, that's ridiculous. Sarah's been mixed up for quite some time and you know it," Maria argued.

"Do you have any children Mr. Clancy?" Maria asked.

"No, I don't, not that I know of," I said.

"You know Mr. Clancy, Johnny is right. I do psychoanalyze people I meet. It's been both a gift and a curse. It has been so much a part of me that sometimes it is hard to switch gears. Come on Mr. Clancy, haven't you heard of people with a sixth sense? We all have it. Some recognize it, while others don't even have a clue. And I'm sure Mr. Clancy with you being a private investigator you must recognize it as well?"

"I suppose you're right Mrs. O'Brien."

"You look as if you're about ready to pass out Mr. Clancy. Are you going to be all right? Perhaps we should be going, eh Johnny? Maria suggested.

"I'm afraid that the early flight, plus the fact I did not get a lot of sleep last night has finally caught up with me. It is awful nice of you to put us up for the night. Thank you very much for your hospitality," I said.

Long Ball took care of the check, and we were just about ready to head out to our cars via the patio steps when I asked everyone. "Do you mind if I go out the main entrance? I collect hats. And there is one I was eyeing when we came in that I would like to get," I said. They all looked at me as if I was crazy.

112

CHAPTER SIX

ROOMS WITH VIEWS

Long Ball pushed the remote button on his key fob and started the car. I couldn't wait to talk to Long Ball in private and be out of earshot of the O'Brien's. They pulled up right next to us as we were getting into the car. Even though Long Ball knew where they lived, we decided to follow them just to be on the safe side. Long Ball's been drinking, and he might be on the borderline where he shouldn't be driving.

"Are you going to be, okay?" I asked.

"I'm fine. Can you believe that girl, talking to her mother like that? If that was my daughter, she'd be getting a whipping. And I would make her go pick me a switch and beat her sorry behind. I don't care how old she is," said Long Ball.

"I followed Sarah when she left to go get her sweater out of the car."

"I know you did. What did you see?"

"She was having a very intense conversation with someone on her cell phone.

She was crying and screaming at the person on the other end," I said.

"Have you known Maria very long? What's up with the voodoo thing with her hands?" I asked.

"I've known her for a few years; ever since Nina started at Stanford. I knew Maria was a little eccentric, but I had no idea she was that far out with the hand business. She's never used it on me for some reason," Long Ball said trying to keep up with the O'Brien's in front of us.

"What about Sarah's response to her mother? Have you ever seen them react like that towards one another? I wish I had an opportunity to ask her some more questions Long Ball. I'm going to talk to Sarah's coach and see if she can be of any help."

"Her eyes really lit up when you asked for the name of her coach. Did you see that?"

"I sure did. You know what got me? When she said, I don't consider you Black."

"I don't know Clancy, just consider the source. You got some naïve rich girl, who doesn't have a clue about anything and has been protected her entire life."

I didn't know I drifted off until Long Ball tapped me on my shoulder as we drove up the driveway and told me, "We're here."

I looked over at the clock on the dash and it read11:35. Sarah's red BMW 330i was already parked in one slot of the four-car garage.

Johnny parked the Benz in the empty slot right next to his daughter's. Johnny got out of the car and pointed for us to park in front of the one garage door that was closed. I stretched and yawned as I got out of the car. The first thing I noticed was that it was a lot cooler, and I could hear the ocean.

"I love listening to the waves as they hit the beach. I find the water very soothing," I said to Long Ball.

"That's probably why you live on the river in Spokane isn't it?"

"Yup."

We walked up the covered breezeway from the garage that led to the back entrance to the house. There was a mudroom that we passed through which led us to the kitchen. Maria was already inside standing at the kitchen sink turning on the faucet and filling up a teapot.

"Would you care for some Chamomile tea Mr. Clancy? It helps you relax. You'll find it quite soothing. I always have a cup before I go to bed," she said.

"I'm so tired right now Mrs. O'Brien I don't think I need it. However, if you insist maybe I will."

"We can have a little chat, Mr. Clancy. Come with me and let me show you around the house while we wait for the water to boil."

Long Ball was off somewhere else with Johnny. I heard pool balls slamming into each other from a distance in another room.

"Where did Long Ball and Johnny go?"

"They are in the game room playing pool," she said.

"You have a gorgeous house, Mrs. O'Brien. How big is it?"

"Thank you, Mr. Clancy. The house is around 6200 square feet. We have six bedrooms, four bathrooms, a den, a game room, and a library."

The kitchen is huge. The cherry cabinets match the color of the hardwood floors. The black granite countertops run along the walls of the kitchen in an L-shape configuration which blends well with the brushed aluminum appliances. Even the Viking Professional six-top stove and convection oven stand out. Martha Stewart would be happy to use it on her cooking show. Mrs. O'Brien has every gadget you'd ever want displayed across the counters. And of course, the can lighting illuminates every part of the working area to perfection, especially the island with a large soapstone counter and farm sink. Mrs. O'Brien was pleased to show me all the special pull-out drawers and cubbyholes she has to store everything. The rest of the house was just as exquisite. The home had everything you would expect to see in Sunset Magazine or

Architectural Digest. "Do your friends call you Martha Stewart?" I asked.

She smiled and said, "Thank you for the compliment."

Mrs. O'Brien led me to the game room just as the teapot started to whistle. She excused herself to go to the kitchen. I started to go with her, but she waved me off.

"Don't worry Mr. Clancy, I'll bring it in here. You stay right here with the boys."

From the looks of it, Johnny and Long Ball were in an intense game of eight-ball.

"You better stick with golf Long Ball," Johnny teased as he made his fifth straight shot.

Long Ball looked dumbfounded. The only shot he took was on the initial break to get the game started.

"Five-ball in the side pocket," Johnny said. By making that shot, Johnny was lined up for the three-ball in the corner pocket. This left him in perfect shape for the eight ball at the opposite corner of the table and the win.

"Usually, winners break, however, I'll make an exception to the rule this time and give you the honors Long Ball since you are a guest," Johnny said.

I never knew Long Ball to get so upset, but he was letting it show. The blue-striped ten-ball slowly rolled into the side pocket after Long Ball's meager attempt at breaking the rack.

Mrs. O'Brien returned with a silver serving tray with two white teacups and a matching teapot. "Let me show you the rest of the house while we let the tea steep for a few minutes," she said.

Just to the right of the game room was a set of cherry wood paneled French doors with a solid glass window in each door. The doors were closed but you could see from the hallway lights that the office was well-equipped with two computer stations for both Mr. and Mrs. O'Brien. On one side was a bookshelf lined with awards, pictures, trophies, and books. I could just make out an image of a miniature pool table attached with some sort of plaque for first place. Poor Long Ball I thought to myself. A peninsula extended out from the center of the bookshelf where a flat-screen computer monitor sat. The same setup was on the opposite side of the office. Matching burgundy leather wingback chairs were at each desk.

Moving right along, Mrs. O'Brien took me to one of her favorite rooms. Another set of French doors, except these doors were solid oak with a cherry wood stain. All the wood trim, doors, floors, and crown molding consisted of this cherry wood stain. There were pocket doors that slid open into the walls. Mrs. O'Brien flicked on the lights that illuminated this magnificent circular library. There was a ladder that was connected to a rail system that ran the entire circumference of the entire room. In the center of the room was this enormous chandelier that hung from the ceiling.

"This is pretty impressive Mrs. O'Brien," I said in awe.

"Thank you, Mr. Clancy."

"Where do the stairs lead?" I asked.

"They go to the loft and the observatory. It's Johnny's hobby. He's been into astronomy for years. When we built the house, Johnny said he always wanted to have a house with an observatory. So now he has his telescope, and he is in seventh heaven."

Continuing straight down the hall from the library we turned to the left, which led us to three bedrooms. Two of the bedroom doors were open with no one occupying them.

"Please be quiet. The middle door is Sarah's room, and she must be asleep by now," whispered Mrs. O'Brien. On the opposite side of the bedrooms were three more wood-paneled glass doors, which led to a courtyard outside. The expansive courtyard had an outdoor fireplace along one side of the wall. The fireplace was surrounded by an array of Adirondack chairs and other patio furniture fixtures. At the end of the hall was an archway, which led back into the kitchen and family room.

"Mr. Clancy, we should head back to the game room, otherwise our tea will be too cold to drink. The other wing of the house has another bedroom, which is the master bedroom and the media center," she explained.

"Well, you certainly have a beautiful home," I told her.

"Thank you, we really enjoy it here."

We went through the kitchen to the other hallway that led to the game room. Long Ball still had an angry defeated look on his face. "How'd you do Long Ball?" I asked.

"I lost both games and I'm ready for bed," Long Ball said sounding frustrated.

"Long Ball I have a confession to make. Since I last saw you, which was two years ago, I joined a pool league. I play in tournaments every Tuesday night," Johnny said.

"I guess that explains the trophies in the office," I said.

"Are you winning any money?" Long Ball asked.

"I'm not making money like you, but I am getting better and hope to qualify for The Players Tournament in Las Vegas. It's a one-million-dollar purse," Johnny said.

"That's great Johnny, I had no idea," Long Ball said.

"Honey, I'm going to bed," John said to Maria. "Long Ball, you remember your way to the guest cottage, don't you?"

"Yes sir."

"Good. It was nice meeting you, Clancy. Your room is above the garage. There is a staircase on the side of the garage," Johnny said.

"It's okay, I'll show him," Maria said to her husband.

As the two men walked off to their separate quarters, Mrs. O'Brien and I had a seat at the pub table where she had placed the tea service earlier. Mrs. O'Brien had already poured the tea into our cups and she was pleased to see that the tea was still hot.

"So, Mr. Clancy, what is your take on Nina's murder?" she asked as she pulled the wooden honey dipper out of the honey jar.

I was surprised she asked me about Nina, I thought she would ask me something more about Tanya. "I don't know why someone would want to kill Nina. She didn't have any enemies that I knew of."

"She was such a sweet girl. Everyone loved her Mr. Clancy."

"Obviously, someone didn't," I said as I took a sip of the tea.

"So how do you feel now that you'll be seeing Tanya tomorrow night?"

"I don't know, I didn't expect to see Tanya this soon."

"What are you afraid of Mr. Clancy?"

"My past I suppose. It's been so long since I've seen her. I don't know what's going to happen. Is she still going to look the same?

121

I really loved that woman. I don't know if she's married, or if she has any kids?"

"How do you think she's going to feel about you? Do you think she may have the same concerns about you?"

"She could, but I doubt it."

"Why is that?"

"Tanya is the one that walked out on me. I wanted to get married. But for some reason, she decided not to. It doesn't make sense."

"I'm sorry to hear that Mr. Clancy."

"I can't think of one thing that changed her mind."

"Well, Mr. Clancy, you will have your chance tomorrow. I hope you find the answers you are searching for," she said as she got up from the table.

"Come with me, I will show you to your room."

We walked through the kitchen to the back door where we came in. There was a pathway that led to the garage. A motion sensor light kicked on just as we reached the bottom of the stairs that led up to the apartment above the garage. There was another path just past the garage which I assumed was the way to the guest cottage where Long Ball was probably snoring away by now. I followed Mrs. O'Brien to the door to the apartment, which she opened. It was beautifully furnished. The small kitchenette had a gas stove, microwave, and a small refrigerator.

A pub table was next to a window with two place settings. A couch and a matching overstuffed leather chair were in the main living area. The chair was positioned right in front of a large-screen TV and coffee table.

"Mr. Clancy, the refrigerator is stocked with food and beverages. If you should need anything else, the back door will be unlocked for you. Your bathroom is down the hallway to the left next to the bedroom. Good night Mr. Clancy."

"Thank you, Mrs. O'Brien," I said as I closed the door behind her. I went inside the bedroom and opened the window to let some cool air come in. The smell of the salt air and the sound of the ocean waves was very relaxing. Before I knew it, I was sound asleep. The sound of my alarm on my cell phone startled me awake as I got up to shut it off. After we left the restaurant, I made sure I set my alarm for 2:45. I didn't bother telling Long Ball what I was planning to do in the middle of the night. I figured everyone should be sound asleep by that time. It was 12:30 when Mrs. O'Brien left my room. I opened the door and saw that there was a full moon, and the sound of the waves was louder. Just as I made my way to the first step, the darn motion light came on. It startled the hell out of me. I hope no one else saw it. I made my way over to the back door and just like Mrs. O'Brien said the door was unlocked.

I opened the door slowly, however, the hinge still squeaked loud enough that I hesitated a minute before I closed it. I wanted to make sure that nobody woke up. I made my way down the hallway of the wing where Sarah's bedroom was located. The other bedroom doors were still open. Ever so gently I turned the doorknob on Sarah's door and pushed it open. I eased my way in between the narrow opening and closed the door just enough so it would not shut completely. I took out my small pen-size flashlight and turned it on. It gave off enough light to help me make my way around her room to find out what I was looking for. Bingo! There it was, right on top of Sarah's nightstand. Sarah had her cell phone plugged into the AC adapter so it could be recharged. I reached over and grabbed the cell phone and disconnected the adapter from it and noticed a set of eyes looking at me. It was a Siamese cat. Thank God, the cat didn't get startled and jump off the bed. Unfortunately, the phone had been turned off. I moved away from the bed towards the door and pushed the power button. The phone came to life, "Thank you for using AT&T."

Fortunately, Sarah was a very sound sleeper, and she didn't even flinch. I started to scroll through the list of recently made calls. Why on earth would she have a telephone number with an area code of 509? I quickly jotted down the number on my notepad and placed the phone back onto the nightstand making sure I plugged the adapter back in.

I closed Sarah's bedroom door and made my way back into the kitchen. I heard footsteps coming down the hallway getting closer to the kitchen. I started to panic. I didn't have time to make it to the door to get out, so I had to think of something quick.

"Oh, Mr. Clancy, you startled me," Mrs. O'Brien said as I filled my coffee mug with water from the automatic dispenser in the refrigerator door.

"I'm sorry Mrs. O'Brien, I didn't mean to wake you up. I was going to make some more tea. I went right to sleep at first, but I woke up and started thinking about Tanya," I said trying to make up some excuse hoping that she would fall for it.

"I couldn't get back to sleep so I decided that maybe another cup of tea might help."

"Mr. Clancy, you didn't have to come all the way down here. I have a fully stocked wooden serving box with a variety of teas in the kitchenette."

"You know I didn't even think of that," I said making my way over to the sink to empty the water from the mug.

"Well good night Mrs. O'Brien. I will talk to you in the morning."

"Good night Mr. Clancy."

Mrs. O'Brien shut the door behind me, and I made my way back up the stairs into my apartment. Boy that was close I said to myself. I better turn the light on and make some tea in case she is watching.

CHAPTER SEVEN

DINNER ANYONE?

Earlier that morning I decided to call Wade before we left. "Wade, it's me, Clancy. I'm sorry to call you so early."

"What's up?" Wade asked.

I told him about our golf outing at Pebble Beach. He was jealous; especially when I told him I shot a 79.

"It turns out that one of our caddies is a friend of Long Ball's. Some guy named Johnny O'Brien," I said to Wade. "Guess what else?"

"Nina and Johnny's daughter, Sarah, were roommates. And Sarah also played on the golf team at Stanford."

"My god, you're kidding me, Clancy?"

"No, not at all. Sarah was ranked number two behind Nina."

"Well, what else happened last night Clancy?"

"Last night I sneaked into Sarah O'Brien's bedroom."

"While she was still in there?"

"Yes."

"What on earth for Clancy? Are you nuts?"

"Listen, let me explain," I told him about dinner last night and Sarah's behavior towards her parents.

"Wade, we were all sitting outside on the patio. Sarah made an excuse to get her sweater out of her car, saying she was cold. I followed her but watched her from inside the restaurant to see what she was up to. Sarah was in the middle of a heated conversation on her cell phone and was rather upset."

"I see, so you felt compelled to follow her home?"

"No, not at all. The O'Brien's invited us to stay at their house instead of driving back to Long Ball's house."

"How convenient for you," Wade said.

"It was perfect. Sarah left the restaurant before we did and was already asleep when we got there. We stayed up for a while. Long Ball and Johnny O'Brien played pool while Mrs. O'Brien gave me a tour of the house. She led me right to Sarah's bedroom."

"So, what were you planning on doing in Sarah's room? Join her in bed or something?" Wade asked laughing.

"Don't be such a stupid idiot. I wanted to find out who Sarah called."

"Did you get the number?"

128

"Yes, I did. Here's the phone number for you Wade. I want you to call from Spokane, so it looks like a local number calling and not one from California. Just in case the person has caller ID. Do you understand? Can you do that for me? The number is 509-555-1212."

"Sure Clancy, I can do that for you, no problem."

"Call me later and let me know what you find out, okay?"

"All right Clancy."

Around ten o'clock that morning, Long Ball, and I were on the road. We thanked Mrs. O'Brien for their hospitality last night and for the breakfast this morning. I thought to myself how lucky I was to come up with that excuse about wanting another cup of tea that Mrs. O'Brien and I had earlier that evening. She bought it. I didn't bother mentioning it to Long Ball.

"Long Ball, I need to go to the crime scene. Do you have time to go over there with me?" I asked.

"Not really Clancy. I need to get to Tommy's house and help him with the funeral arrangements. But I can do this. How would you like to borrow my Harley?"

"The Road King?"

"Yes," said Long Ball.

"That would be fantastic!" I told him. Long Ball dropped me off at his house and gave me the keys to the Harley. Just as I was getting on the bike, I got a call from Wade.

"Guess what Clancy? The number belongs to Pete Williams," Wade said.

"Are you sure?"

"Absolutely. I called from a payphone. I did not speak with him directly. There was no answer, but it did go into his voicemail. And it was his voice on the recording."

"Where on earth did you find a payphone?"

"The bowling alley by my house still has one."

"How are those two connected?" I asked Wade.

"Beats me Clancy, that doesn't make any sense at all," Wade said.

"Excellent job Wade."

"Thanks, all in a day's work. Are you still with Long Ball?"

"No, he dropped me off at his house. He's on his way to Sausalito to meet with his brother."

"How are you getting around?"

"Long Ball let me use his Harley."

"Man, it must be nice. Clancy, I'll see you at the funeral."

"Thanks again."

I put Long Ball's motorcycle helmet on and started this beautiful machine. I haven't felt this much power between my legs since Tanya. It was a gorgeous day, and it was nice to be back on a bike again. It's been a long time since I rode a motorcycle. The short ride over to Palo Alto is just what I needed. Besides the usual traffic delays the Bay Area is known for was no problem this time of day as I rode over to Wild Creek Golf Course. It looked like a nice track to play. People were looking at me as an oddball riding up on a Harley. Hey, most golf courses rent clubs for patrons to use. Just because I didn't drive up in a Mercedes doesn't mean you should judge me, does it? Looking around it seems like that's what every other car is in the parking lot. I left the helmet and black riding gloves with the bike. I went inside the pro shop to talk with the head pro.

"Excuse me. Sir, I would like to speak with the head pro. Could you please tell me who that is?" I asked.

"Sure thing. It's Bob Clark, I'll get him for you. He's upstairs in the office," he said. "What company are you with sir?" he asked. He was making his way over to the staircase and realized that he should probably tell his boss who was coming to see him. "And, what's your name sir?"

"Clancy, Harry Clancy. Tell him not to worry, I'm not a salesman," I said.

I made my way around the pro shop looking at all the golf clubs, golf balls, clothing, shoes, and all the paraphernalia items they had strategically located to entice you to make a purchase. I tried a couple of putters on their

Astroturf putting green while I waited for Mr. Clark to come down.

"Sir, how may I help you today? My name is Bob Clark. My assistant told me you were not a salesman. Well, if you're not a salesman, what can I do for you? Do you need help with your game?" he asked.

Mr. Clark was a large jovial individual about 5'10". His mustache made him look like he could be senior pro golfer, Craig Stadler's twin brother.

"Mr. Clark, I definitely could use some help with my game. Unfortunately, that's not why I'm here. I'm a private investigator and I would like to talk to you about Nina Jackson's murder if you don't mind?" I asked.

"I don't mind at all. What did you say your name was again? Mr. What?"

"It's Clancy, Harry Clancy," I said.

"Is that Irish or something?"

"Yes, it is," I said.

"But Mr. Clancy, you're the farthest thing from an Irishman I have ever seen," he said.

I figure I better handle this gentlemanly instead of going off on this cracker from Mississippi. "My father was from Ireland and my mother was from Jamaica."

"Boy, you sound like you got a whole heap of people mixed up in your gene pool," he said.

"Do you mind Mr. Clark if we could move on and answer some of my questions?"

132

"Between you and the police, I've told this story about half a dozen times already. Manuel Garcia found Nina's body. He's the greenskeeper. He found Nina's body right over there on the ninth green," he said pointing out the window from the pro shop.

"Do you know what time that was?" I asked.

"I believe it was right around 5:00, no, maybe 5:30 that morning."

"Are you sure about the time?"

"Absolutely."

"How's that?"

"I open up every morning around 5:00. However, that morning, for some reason I left my keys back at the house and I had to double back and go get them. I got here at 5:30. As soon as I unlocked the door, Manuel barged in and told me that there was a dead body on the ninth green."

"Can you show me where he found the body?"

"Sure, right this way," he said.

We walked outside and waited for the foursome to finish with their putts before we went over to the green where Mr. Garcia found Nina.

"Mr. Clark, the ninth green is relatively close to the clubhouse. Are you surprised that no one else saw the killer discard the body on the green?"

"No, not really."

133

"What about the rest of the crew?"

"I can't answer for the rest of them, Mr. Clancy. You may want to ask the superintendent, Jorge Rodriguez," he suggested.

"He's someone on my list to speak with. How about Mr. Garcia? Is he available?"

"Mr. Clancy, you're not going to believe this. Mr. Garcia quit that very day her body was found."

"Are you serious Mr. Clark?

"Yes sir."

"That had to be right after his interview with the news reporter," I said.

"We were all shocked, he was a good worker. But you are right, he did quit right then and there."

"Mr. Clark, could you point me in the right direction where I might find the superintendent?" I asked as we made our way back to the pro shop.

"The maintenance yard is just down the service road over yonder," he said pointing at one of the maintenance carts going over there.

I started to walk over that way when he stopped me.

"It's not going to do you any good today. It's his day off. He will be here tomorrow morning," Mr. Clark said.

"Thank you very much for your help today," I said as we stopped at the door of the pro shop. "One more question Mr. Clark. What part of Mississippi are you from?"

"Well, don't that beat all? How did you know I was from Mississippi?"

"Let's just say, you still have your accent, and besides, someone of your stature must come from the Deep South," I said.

"Actually, I'm from Tupelo. You know what they say, Mr. Clancy. You can take the boy out of the country, but you can't take the country out of the boy."

I said goodbye to Mr. Clark and thanked god I didn't have to see him again. I wanted to ask him when the next Klan meeting is, I'm sure he knows where the local chapter is in Northern California.

I decided to make my way over to the Palo Alto Police Department to see what I could find out about Manuel Garcia. I figure it would be a good time for me to do that since Mr. Rodriguez won't be at work until tomorrow. Nina's funeral is the next day. There is no way I'll be able to go there after the service. I must see him tomorrow. This means I'm going to have to get up early to see the superintendent. It will be a busy day.

I pulled into the parking lot of the Palo Alto Police Department and found a spot for motorcycles. I took a deep breath and asked myself if I was ready to meet Tanya as I walked into the entrance. "May I help you sir?" the female officer asked me as I approached the information desk.

"Yes, you may. I am looking for Detective Tanya Jones. Is she in?" I asked.

"I'll ring her office. Whom shall I say is calling?"

"Harry Clancy."

"Have a seat, Mr. Clancy, someone will be right with you," she said as she hung up the telephone.

After a few minutes of leafing through several magazines, a door finally opens. My heart was pounding. I didn't know what to say or how to react. Instead of seeing this beautiful woman, I hear this tall blond guy calling out my name, "Clancy, Harry Clancy."

"That's me I said.

He comes over to me and shakes my hand. He introduces himself, "I'm Detective Joe Bowman. I'm Tanya's partner. Unfortunately, she is not in right now. What can I help you with?" he asked.

"I'm here to see Tanya if you don't mind?"

"I understand Mr. Clancy, we work together. Perhaps I may be of service to you," he suggested.

Detective Bowman stretched his ID badge with a retractable cord and waved it in front of the control panel located near the door. The latch opened and we went inside and walked down a long corridor leading to the main office. We were on the other side of the counter, which separates us from the booking area.

136

The bulletproof glass ran down the whole length of the counter protecting the desk sergeant. He spoke through an intercom to a couple of officers who had some Asian guy in handcuffs. Detective Bowman led me down another hallway to an area with gray cubicles for offices. A bunch of suits were walking around as he stopped in front of one of the cubicles with his nameplate on the entrance to his office.

"Please have a seat, Mr. Clancy," he said motioning me to sit down with his hand. "How may I help you?"

My better judgment told me not to say anything about the case; instead, I opened my big fat mouth. "I went over to Wild Creek Golf Course to talk with the head pro about Nina Jackson's murder. I wanted to ask the pro some questions about the greenskeeper, Manuel Garcia, who found Nina's body. The pro told me that Mr. Garcia quit the same day that Nina's body was found. I thought that was a little odd. I wanted to ask Tanya if she knew anything about this guy Garcia. And that's the reason I came over here," I said.

"Well first off, tell me why I should share information on a case with you?" Detective Bowman asked.

I took out one of my business cards and handed it over to Detective Bowman. Joe read the card and said," A private investigator! Even more reason for me not to help you."

"Listen, I was hired by Al Jackson, Nina's uncle, to find her killer."

"And?"

"I want your help. I need your help."

I knew it was a big mistake talking to this jerk, I said to myself. He's being very uncooperative. "Can you do me a favor?" I asked.

"What's that?"

"Could you please give Tanya my business card and have her call me?" I asked as I got up to leave.

"Sure, no problem, I can do that for you," Detective Bowman said as he escorted me back to the information desk. I winked at the officer behind the information counter as I left. "Thank you for your help," I said.

She smiled and said, "Have a nice day Mr. Clancy."

She's a little cutie I said to myself as I walked outside to the parking lot and over to the Harley. I was just about to start the motorcycle when the officer from the information desk came over to me and said, "Mr. Clancy, please wait."

"What is it, officer?" I asked.

"Do you have another business card? I saw Detective Bowman throw your business card into the trashcan after you left Mr. Clancy."

"He did what?" I asked as I pulled another card out of my pocket and handed it to her.

"Yes, he did Mr. Clancy. Detective Bowman can be a real Richard Cranium at times," she said.

"What do you mean, Richard Cranium?"

"A dickhead Mr. Clancy," she said.

"Who are you?" I asked.

"I'm sorry. I'm Officer Blake, Officer Theresa Blake."

"Nice to meet you, Officer Blake," I said. "Will you see that my card gets to Detective Tanya Jones?" I asked.

"I'm off right now. Please call me Theresa," she said with a sultry voice that matched those luscious lips of hers.

"Nice to meet you, Theresa," I said as I extended my hand to shake hers.

"Mr. Clancy, would you like to join me for a drink?" she asked.

I looked at my watch and said, "Just one drink."

"Give me five minutes and I'll meet you right back here," she said walking off to the employee parking lot.

After a few minutes, a burgundy BMW motorcycle approaches. I had to do a double-take when I realized it was Officer Blake. She was wearing a black leather jacket, boots, and chaps.

"Follow me, Mr. Clancy," she said. Moments later, we pulled into the parking lot at the Park-Inn Tavern. I noticed quite a few bikes in the parking lot. We got off our bikes and took off our helmets. Officer Blake looked so good in that leather outfit she was wearing. It looks like it was glued on.

"You sure are full of surprises," I said as we made our way inside.

"You haven't seen anything yet Mr. Clancy."

We made our way over to a booth and sat down. A waitress with pink hair, a nose ring, a pierced tongue, and an array of rings in her ears and eyebrows came over to take our order. The tattoo of a dragon that ran down the entire length of her right arm completed her ensemble.

"Hey Theresa, what can I get for you girl?" she asked.

"A pitcher of beer and an order of hot wings sounds good," Theresa said.

"Did you want anything Mr. Clancy?" she asked.

"No, that's fine. I don't understand, why did you order a whole pitcher if I'm going to have one drink?" I asked.

"Not to worry Mr. Clancy. My partner is coming to meet me, and she'll help us drink it."

"Okay."

Just as the waitress was leaving, Theresa asked about her partner, "Have you seen Lucy yet?" "She's on her way, she should be here soon," Pinkie said.

"Officer Blake, I got to ask you this question. Has anyone ever told you that you look like Halle Berry?"

"I get it all the time. I've had people come up and ask me for my autograph."

Pinkie made her way back over to our table with our pitcher and three glasses.

"Officer Blake, can I ask you another question?"

"Sure, but please call me Theresa."

"Fair enough if you call me Clancy. All my friends do. I used to be a cop myself. How is it if you're working in an administrative position within the police department that you have a partner?" Theresa didn't even have a chance to open her mouth to give me an answer. A beautiful Asian woman came over to Theresa and planted a wet one across her lips.

"Clancy, this is my partner Lucy Lin. Lucy, this is Mr. Harry Clancy. He is a private investigator. He stopped by the station this afternoon," she explained.

"Nice to meet you, Mr. Clancy," Lucy said sliding into the booth next to Theresa.

"Nice to meet you too Lucy," I said hoping the shocked look on my face wasn't that obvious. At that moment, I looked around the entire bar and realized that I was the only man inside this gay women's bar.

"Clancy, Lucy is the owner of the Park-Inn," Theresa said.

141

"That's nice. Have you owned it very long?" I asked.

"About five years."

"Lovely place," I said.

Thank God Pinkie made her way back over with our order of wings. I needed to put something else in my mouth besides my foot.

"Mr. Clancy, do you live here in the Bay Area?" Lucy asked.

"No, I'm from the Pacific Northwest, Spokane, Washington," I said.

"Doesn't it rain a lot up there?"

"Not as bad as Seattle, which is on the other side of the state. Spokane is on the other side of the Cascade Mountain Range close to the Idaho border where it doesn't rain as much," I said.

"What brings you down here?" Lucy asked.

"You must have heard about that coed that was found murdered a few days ago at Wild Creek Golf Course, didn't you?"

"No, I didn't hear anything about it," Lucy said.

"Sure, you did Lucy, remember I told you about her? She was that girl from Stanford. Detective Jones and I were talking about her the other day," Theresa said.

"Oh, that girl," Lucy said as she took a sip of her beer.

"I was hired by her uncle to help find the killer. I've known Nina since she was a little girl. Nina is the fourth Black golfer to be murdered in

142

the past several months. Her uncle, Al Jackson, not only hired me to find her killer, but to provide protection for him as well," I explained to them as I got up to leave.

"I'm sorry Clancy, I'll make sure Tanya gets your card tomorrow," Theresa said.

"Thank you for your help, Theresa."

"Mr. Clancy, please come back again and visit us," Lucy said.

"I will," I said making my way over to the door. I glanced back at the two of them as I was going out. They were in another lip lock swapping saliva.

I made my way over to the 101. The traffic was so backed up it would take forever to get to Tommy's house. It would be worse if I was in a car. Then it dawned on me; you can ride between the lanes here in California with a motorcycle. I realized that when I saw another guy on a bike doing just that. He was weaving right in between traffic. It looks dangerous as hell. But I noticed I could probably knock off an hour of my commute over to Sausalito by doing this. I'm almost there and I don't mind going through San Francisco. It's been a long time since I've been to the city. I wish I had time to go down to Fisherman's Wharf and get some seafood.

I'm glad I decided to put my jacket on before I left the girls at the Park-Inn. The temperature dropped almost twenty degrees once I got into the city; even in the middle of summer.

The traffic was backed up at the Golden Gate Bridge; especially in the southbound lanes going back into the city. Thank goodness, I was going in the opposite direction. San Francisco is one of the most beautiful places in the world; it's too bad that it is so bloody expensive to live here. Plus, the traffic is a bear. Thank God, I live in God's country. It would take a miracle for me to ever live in California. And Southern California is out of the question.

I was finally able to make some headway once traffic started moving over the bridge. Thank goodness, I've been over to Tommy's house before. Riding a motorcycle and looking at directions at the same time would make it rather difficult for me. I don't think I could multitask that well. I made a right turn on San Gabriel and left on Santa Maria looking for 4130. Let's see 3960, 3982, 4020 and finally 4130. Long Ball's Maserati and Tommy's Land Rover were parked in the driveway. A couple of other cars were doubled up behind the Land Rover and Maserati. There was no room for another car to park close to their house. I hope Tommy doesn't mind me parking Long Ball's motorcycle on the sidewalk. Fortunately, someone was coming out of the house ready to leave. They were walking over to a black Jetta, which was parked right next to the driveway. I could tell when I got off the bike that I was going to be a little saddle-sore tomorrow. I made my way up the walkway and the steps leading to their terracotta tile front porch. The porch wrapped around to the rear of the Mediterranean style two-story home. Just as I was about to ring the doorbell another group of people were leaving. Tommy's wife Brenda was escorting them out the door.

"Hi Harry, thank you so much for coming. Al told us you flew in yesterday and that you would be stopping by," she said as she gave me a hug. "You look well Harry."

"Brenda, you look gorgeous as ever," I said to her as we made our way inside. Brenda is 5'10" coffee colored, with just a little bit of cream. She wore her hair in natural braids that were shoulder length and tied in a ponytail. Being the perfect hostess, she is known for, she wore a cream-colored pantsuit, accented with some beautiful African jewelry. The one thing about Brenda, she will never have a single hair out of place. Everything she wears matches perfectly. I suppose she got that from her years of being a model with the Ford Agency in New York. Brenda was on the cover of Vogue, Cosmopolitan, and others.

Working for the agency is how she met Tommy. Before coming to San Francisco, Tommy worked for an ad agency. Brenda did some layouts for a cosmetic company which was one of Tommy's accounts. They fell in love at first sight. Eventually, deciding to get married.

Unfortunately, Brenda's father was ill, and they had to move to Spokane to help her mother. Both their careers were taking off, but they had to do what was right. They ended up staying in Spokane for a year.

"Harry, is that you?" Tommy came running up to me and gave me a great big bear hug which knocked the wind out of me as he slapped me on my back. Tommy wore a pair of khaki pants and matching brown leather deck shoes. He wore a rather colorful Hawaiian shirt, which was hanging over his protruding belly.

"Tommy, how are you doing?" I asked realizing that's got to be the dumbest question to ask someone who will be burying his daughter in a few days.

"Clancy, all things considered, we're doing fine," he said putting his arm around his wife.

"Tommy, you look like you haven't missed too many meals," I said.

"Don't go there," Tommy said.

"Hey Clancy, how did you like riding the Road King? Pretty nice huh?" Long Ball asked as he made his way to the foyer over to us.

"Very smooth ride. Thanks, for letting me use it," I said as Brenda and Tommy took me inside to introduce me to some more family members.

"Let me grab you a beer Clancy, I'll be right back," Long Ball said.

About 25 people were roaming throughout the house dropping off food and drinks for the family. While others made their way into the kitchen; helping themselves with a to-go plate and wrapping it in aluminum foil. That's Black folks for you. They have no shame.

Brenda took considerable pride in her house. The circular foyer has sand-colored tiles with black marble diamond shape inlays in the middle, which makes a large star-shaped design. A brown iron chandelier hangs twelve feet from the top of the cathedral ceiling. Brenda has everything in place. Various pieces of African art decorate the shelves and alcoves throughout their home. Several pieces Brenda and Tommy brought back from Kenya. Just to the left of the foyer is the dining room. The table is formally set for ten people.

Brenda came over to me and said, "We'll be kicking some of the people out of here soon so we can eat. I told everyone that we're going to have a private meal with the family."

"I understand, I will leave soon and make my way back over to Long Ball's house," I said.

"Where the hell do you think you're going, Harry? Are you crazy? You are family. Besides, Long Ball invited someone to come over that he wants you to meet," she said.

"Thank you," I said remembering that Long Ball invited Tanya over.

"Here's your beer Clancy," Long Ball said as he handed it to me.

"I wish you didn't invite Tanya to dinner Long Ball," I said.

"Don't worry, you will thank me later," he said smiling.

We made our way into the kitchen and the family room. The tile from the foyer and hallway stopped at the entrance to the kitchen. The floors in the kitchen were cherry wood. The floors matched the cherry wood cabinets. Suspended above the black granite island is a stainless-steel rack that hangs from the ceiling with gourmet pots and pans hanging from it. The island is large enough to have six people sit comfortably at the counter, which four men and two women were doing as they devoured a helping of chicken wings and potato salad. They looked as if they did not want anyone interrupting their feeding frenzy as Brenda and I walked by and made our way into the family room. The floor-to-ceiling windows made the view of the San Francisco Bay more breathtaking. A couple of guys were glued to the 80-inch LED 4K Ultra HD TV and erupted in a loud cheer as a player for the San Francisco Giants hit another game-winning bottom of the ninth walk-off home run.

The end of the game signaled it was time to leave. People made their way to the front door and left. The only ones left behind were family members from Atlanta who were staying with

Tommy and Brenda, as well as Long Ball and myself. I made my way through the house with a plastic trash bag and picked up some of the plates and glasses. I took the overstuffed plastic bag outside and dumped it into the garbage can on the side of the house. Back inside Brenda took out the prime rib from the oven along with the baked potatoes and set them on the island.

"Please join us in the dining room, dinner is about to be served," Tommy announced to everyone. Long Ball and I brought the rest of the food into the dining room. Plates were being passed around as Tommy placed sliced portions of the prime rib on them. Long Ball walked around the table filling glasses with a nice Merlot for those who wanted some.

"I want to thank you all for coming here today. It is a sad time in our lives that brings you all here. Nina brought such joy to our hearts. I was blessed to be her father. Our children are supposed to bury us, not for us to bury them. God, please bless this food which we are about to receive and for the fellowship. To Nina, Amen," Tommy said with his voice breaking up as tears streamed down his face.

"To Nina," we all said quietly in unison.

The doorbell rang and Long Ball looked at his watch as if expecting someone. He got up to answer the door and motioned Brenda to stay seated. I just about choked on my piece of prime rib when I looked up and saw Tanya Jones walking in with Long Ball. I gave an angry glance over to Long Ball who was smiling and said, "I got you."

I immediately got up and excused myself and headed off to the bathroom without saying a word to Tanya, as I heard Long Ball introducing her to everyone at the dinner table. I struggled to throw water on my face to calm myself down. I didn't know what to expect when I saw her. It was supposed to be in a more controlled environment like the police station, I said to myself looking in the bathroom mirror.

Thinking that I finally had everything under control, I came back out to join the group, only to find Tanya sitting in the chair next to me. I extended my hand to shake hers, which seemed awkward. However, her touch sent a bolt of energy through me that I hadn't felt in years. It was so strong that I didn't want to let go. Instead, I felt compelled to hug her. At that moment, it felt as if we went back in time when we first met. Her eyes were so mesmerizing; my knees became weak every time I gazed into them. It was like magic.

"Hello Harry, you look wonderful," Tanya said breaking away from our hug, bringing me back to reality.

"So do you Tanya, so do you," I said with my heart racing as if I was running the 100-meter dash. Eight sets of eyes were silently looking at us waiting to hear the next words to come out of our mouths.

I started to ask Tanya, "Why did you leave me hanging like that at the altar?" But she put her finger to my lips to stop me.

"In time Harry, in time, this is not the place," she said, as the silence was broken when everyone went back to shoveling food into their mouths.

I had to take inventory of her beauty. Tanya was stunning. She wore a black pantsuit with a white blouse. Her shoulder length thick straight black hair was tied in a ponytail. I've always loved Tanya's hair. She could wear it in so many different styles. I especially liked it when she wore it in a French Twist. No need for a weave with her. Tanya was easy on the eyes. Very light skinned with those doe-like brown eyes. They look a lot nicer in person than seeing them on TV. Finally, her body. Tanya filled out her 5'8 frame perfectly, with ample breasts, long legs, luscious lips, and not an ounce of fat on her. She was cut to perfection.

"Tanya is one of the detectives working on the case," Long Ball explained to the family.

Tommy and Brenda perked right up when they heard that news from Long Ball. They were eager to find out if Tanya had any information to share with them.

"My wife and I are so grief-stricken at our loss, which I'm sure you can understand. Do you

151

have any leads or any idea who killed our baby?" Tommy asked as Brenda placed her hand on top of his left hand.

"I don't have much to go on," Tanya said to the family. "I can understand your eagerness to find out who murdered your daughter," Tanya said sympathetically. "I can assure you that the Palo Alto Police Department is doing everything possible to find out who caused this dreadful incident to happen to you," she said.

"Tommy, I went to the murder scene earlier today at Wild Creek and spoke with the head pro today," I said.

"Did you find anything out?" Tommy eagerly asked.

"Yes, I did Tommy. Manuel Garcia is the greenskeeper who found Nina's body. He also quit that very day," I said.

"That's it, that's all you found out?" Tommy asked in disbelief.

"Unfortunately, the superintendent, who is Manuel Garcia's boss was off this afternoon. I plan on going back out to the golf course tomorrow to find out what he can tell me about the crime scene. Perhaps the Palo Alto P.D., will be so kind as to join me tomorrow and help me with my investigation?" I asked.

"I promise you Mr. and Mrs. Jackson, I will help Harry in his investigation. But, please keep in mind, that this is in our jurisdiction," Tanya said getting up to leave who is visibly upset with

152

Harry for putting her on the spot. "Thank you for inviting me, Al. Good night Mr. and Mrs. Jackson," she said.

"I'll see you out Tanya," Brenda said to her.

"No need, I can find my way out," she said.

I sat there in silence for a moment trying to figure out what happened when Long Ball said, "You better get off your black ass and go after her, you, stupid idiot."

I got up and ran outside to her car just as she was ready to get in, "Tanya, please wait. Look, I haven't seen you in twenty-four years. You owe me an explanation," I said.

"Is this what this is all about? You want to find out why I jilted you?"

"Tanya, I saw you on TV the other day. I was at the golf course when the news report came on about Nina's murder. I looked up and saw your face. I didn't plan on meeting you like this. Long Ball pulled a fast one on me. I would not put you in a situation like this at all. Didn't Long Ball tell you I was here?"

"He did tell me that you would be here. I thought I could handle it, but I didn't know what to expect."

"So, you were just as shocked as I was?"

"Absolutely," she said.

Tanya seemed to be cooling down a bit and asked me, "What did you find out today?"

153

"Like I said earlier. I met with the head pro, who told me about Manuel Garcia. I just thought that it was odd that he quit so soon after the murder. Check this out, Mr. Garcia only worked at the golf course for three weeks. It doesn't make sense does it, Tanya?"

"You're right about that Harry?"

"Didn't you know that he quit?" I asked.

"No, I didn't."

"Did you speak with the superintendent?"

"Who, Mr. Rodriguez? Of course, we did. He told me that Manuel Garcia had just started working for them. As far as we were concerned, he was still employed with Wild Creek by the time we left. We never went back to ask more questions."

"No one at Wild Creek called you to let you know that Mr. Garcia quit?"

"No."

"Something is missing here," I said to Tanya. "Will you come with me tomorrow so we can pay a visit to Mr. Rodriguez?" I asked.

"That sounds like a good idea Harry," she said.

"Tanya, I stopped by the station today and met your partner, Joe Bowman. He certainly is a piece of work. How did you get stuck with him?" I asked.

"It's a long story," she explained.

"Did he even tell you that I came by?"

"All he said was, that some Private Dick came by to see me."

"Private Dick?"

"I'm quoting Detective Bowman."

"That idiot! He didn't tell you who I was. That explains a lot. The officer at the information desk told me that he ripped up my business card and threw it in the trash."

"Officer Blake?"

"Yes, that's the one. She's the one who told me. I met her and her girlfriend, partner, lover, or whatever you want to call her at the Park-Inn Tavern this afternoon."

"You must mean Lucy," she said.

"Yes, Lucy Lin. She's cute. So is Theresa. Too bad they only like girls."

"Too bad for them or too bad for you Harry?"

"Too bad for me, well not exactly me. It just seems like such a waste."

"Well, I see you haven't changed much. You're still a dog," she said.

"Who are you calling a dog?" I asked. "You're the one who left me hanging at the altar. Why did you leave me?" I asked, grabbing her arms with both of my hands.

"Look Harry, I know I owe you an explanation, but I'm not ready to get into that right now with you. I'm just as shocked as you are to see me as I am about seeing you too. I am going through a lot of emotions right now as

155

well. Harry, I loved you so much. I didn't want to hurt you. Listen, I'll meet you tomorrow. Come by the precinct in the morning," she said getting into her car and driving off.

CHAPTER EIGHT

TRUST ME

After Tanya left, I went back inside and got the third degree from everyone. They all wanted to know why I let someone that beautiful get away from me. I had to remind them that she left me. I was the one that was jilted not her. I stayed a few more hours at Tommy's house and told Long Ball how upset I was about his little surprise. Even though I was upset at first, I must admit; it was nice to see her.

"Clancy, please stay with us tonight," Brenda said.

"Thank you, Brenda, I appreciate the offer, but all my clothes are at Long Ball's house, and I don't want to fight the morning traffic," I said. "Besides, I'm meeting with Tanya at the police station tomorrow morning," I said, which brought a smile to Brenda's face.

It was 10:00 by the time I got to Long Ball's house. Long Ball decided to stay with his brother. I grabbed a beer out of the refrigerator and made myself comfortable in his easy chair.

I placed my feet on the ottoman and flicked on the large-screen TV. Before I knew it, I was gone. I got up around seven the next morning, still in the easy chair and still in my clothes. The Today Show was on as Al Roker was doing the morning weather roundup across the country. I felt energized and well-rested. I can't remember the last time I slept for nine hours. I went upstairs to my room and pulled out my running gear from my suitcase.

The morning air was cool, and the light marine layer had not completely burned off yet. I'm glad I put on my sweats. I did some stretches on his front porch trying to limber up before I started. I felt an unfamiliar pain coming from my inner thighs. I'm a little saddle sore from riding the Harley. There is a high school a few blocks away from Long Ball's house. I jogged my way over to the track to do a few laps. Fortunately, school's out for the summer and I wouldn't embarrass myself in front of the whole student body. Surprisingly, the school had a dirt track, which made it easy on my knees. I popped off one mile and felt good and I decided to do another one. This feels good, just what I needed. I made my final lap completing three miles in twenty-six minutes. An eight-forty pace is not bad considering I haven't gone running in a month. I did some more stretching to cool down and walked back to Long Ball's house.

After showering and getting cleaned up I rode over to the Palo Alto Police Department. The large clock on the wall behind the information desk read 9:45.

"Good morning Mr. Clancy. How are you today?" Officer Blake asked as I approached the counter.

"I'm well, and yourself?" I asked.

"I'm afraid I might have drunk too much with Lucy last night," she said.

"Make sure you drink a lot of water today to flush the toxins out of your system," I told her. "Could you ring Detective Tanya Jones for me? She is expecting me this time," I said.

"I know she is," Officer Blake said. 'Tanya came in, I mean Detective Jones came in all excited this morning, just like you Mr. Clancy. Tanya told me what happened last night at dinner."

"Did she say anything about me?" I asked.

"All she said was that it was nice seeing you again."

"That's it?"

"Yes sir. Let me ring her for you," Officer Blake said as she buzzed Tanya's line. "Detective Jones, Mr. Harry Clancy is at the information desk waiting to see you," she said hanging up the phone.

"Detective Jones will be right with you."

"Thank you, Officer Blake."

159

The secured door to the back offices opens and out walks Detective Joe Bowman and Detective Tanya Jones. Tanya looked different than she did last night. Her hair was in a French Twist which she knows I like, and she wore a little more makeup. Her gray suit was more professional than the outfit she wore yesterday. The matching skirt showed off her long muscular legs. I wonder if she has them insured for a million dollars like Tina Turner, I said to myself. Then there was Lumpy, Detective Bowman.

"Good morning, Harry, right on time," Tanya said. "You remember my partner, Detective Bowman, don't you?" she asked.

"Yes, I do," I said reluctantly shaking Detective Bowman's hand.

"Detective Bowman has something he wants to say to you, Harry. Isn't that right Joe?" she asked.

"I'm sorry about yesterday. Tanya explained to me this morning that you were her ex-fiancé. Again, I'm sorry," Detective Bowman said, shaking my hand another time.

"No problem detective," I said. You should have seen the look on Officer Blake's face when she overheard everything about me and Tanya.

"Tanya, did you get a chance to tell your partner about my visit with the head pro at Wild Creek?" I asked.

"I briefly filled him in on it and told him that we are going back to talk with the superintendent today," she said.

"Do you want to come with us Detective Bowman?" I asked.

"Not really, I don't want to be the third wheel, Mr. Clancy," he said.

"Joe, I'll fill you in after we visit with Mr. Rodriguez," Tanya said.

"Sure, no problem. I have some paperwork to take care of anyway" he said walking back over to the office door.

Officer Blake buzzed Detective Bowman in before he had time to swipe his magnetic ID card.

"Bye-bye you two," Officer Blake said smiling as we left out the front entrance.

"Do you want to ride with me, or do you want to drive?" I asked.

"Harry, I don't think riding on the back of a Harley with a skirt on would be appropriate. Besides, I don't think you would want me to mess up my French Twist, now, would you?" she asked.

"You remembered, didn't you?"

"Of course, I did," Tanya said.

"Let's have the government pay our way over to Wild Creek. My car is over this way," Tanya said pointing over to the parking lot where all the squad cars and unmarked cars are kept.

I went over to the driver's side and opened the car door for Tanya.

"What do you think you're doing?" she asked.

"I'm opening the car door for you. What does it look like?" I asked.

"Harry, I'm on duty. Don't open my car door for me as if we are on a date. Then it would be a different story," she said.

"Sorry, can we pretend it's a date?"

"You're pushing it, Harry," Tanya said as she slid into the car.

"Tanya, you are so beautiful. Are you seeing anyone?" I asked.

"Not really, I haven't gone out on a date for so long that I forgot what it's like. I never really have the time to get serious with anyone. I have other more important priorities to address."

"What about you Harry? Are you seeing anyone?'

"Me neither Tanya. Ever since you left me, I have felt betrayed. I couldn't trust anyone. I didn't want to get hurt like that again."

"Harry, trust me. I am sorry for what I did to you. I have my reasons."

"What reasons?" I pleaded.

"Harry, I can't tell you right now. Maybe, you're coming down here might bring some closure to it," she said as we pulled into the entrance to Wild Creek Golf Course.

We drove down the service road to the maintenance services building that my friend from Tupelo, Mississippi showed me. The service facility is a Quonset hut-shaped building painted green. The building has a service garage door which was open. Inside, there were maintenance vehicles, golf carts, and riding lawnmowers. A couple of guys inside were tinkering with one of the riding mowers. Tanya parked right next to the steps that lead up to a screen door with a sign above it that said Office. We walked up the steps and knocked on the door, Tanya asked, "Anybody home?"

"What do you want?" a male voice asked.

"We're here to see Jorge Rodriguez," Tanya said.

"That's me, come on in," he said not standing up to meet us.

"Mr. Rodriguez, I'm Detective Jones with the Palo Alto Police Department and this is Harry Clancy."

Tanya didn't know exactly how to introduce me. I didn't have to worry about that, Mr. Rodriguez knew all about me.

"You're that private investigator that was nosing around here yesterday. Bob told me all about you," Mr. Rodriguez said.

"Okay, if that's the way you want to look at it, Jorge, that's fine with me," I said knowing that we were going to have some fun with this clown.

163

"How long have you worked for Wild Creek?" I asked.

"Almost ten years," he said.

Jorge was a little fat guy with dark tanned skin. He must have worked his way through the ranks working outside in the summer as a greenskeeper. From the looks of it, he must be on a power trip as well. We were interrupted by one of his workers who came in to ask him a question.

"Get the hell out of here! Can't you see I'm busy?"

"Are you having a bad day Jorge?" I asked.

"I am now, since you two showed up," he said. "What do you want?"

"Mr. Rodriguez, I want to ask you some questions about Manuel Garcia," Tanya said.

"Go right ahead detective," he said.

"How long did Mr. Garcia work for you?" she asked.

"Manuel just started working for us about three or four weeks ago," he said.

"Was he a good worker?" Tanya asked.

"He was one of my better workers. Always on time, worked late if I needed him."

"Don't you find it odd that he quit right after he found Nina Jackson's body?" Tanya asked.

"I'm sorry to see him go. I'm not surprised that he left. Look, people come and go all the time," he said.

"Do you have much turnover, Jorge?" I asked knowing that he must be an ass to work for.

"We have our fair share," he said.

"Was he legal to work in the U.S. Mr. Rodriguez?" Tanya asked.

"Yes, he was a U.S. citizen," he said.

"Mr. Rodriguez, I would like to see the employee records for Mr. Garcia if you don't mind?" she asked.

"No way, I'm not at liberty to do that," he said.

"Are you refusing to show me his records Mr. Rodriguez?" she asked.

"Yes."

"I'm sorry to hear that Mr. Rodriguez. I can get a search warrant and close the course down or you can cooperate with the Palo Alto P.D. Now, what do you want to do?" Tanya asked pulling out her cell phone.

"Do you want me to call and get a search warrant?"

"Hold on a minute, let me call Bob. He has to authorize it," he said as he picked up the phone and called.

"There's a detective from the Palo Alto P.D.; and the private investigator that was here yesterday. She wants to see the employee records for Manuel Garcia. If I don't give it to her, she said she would close the course down. What do you want me to do? Yes sir, I understand," Jorge said hanging up the phone.

"What did he say, Jorge?" I asked.

"He said for me to give them to you."

Reluctantly, Mr. Rodriguez went over to the filing cabinet and pulled out a file folder with the contact information for Manuel Garcia. "Here you go detective," Mr. Rodriguez said handing the file to Tanya.

"Thank you so much, Mr. Rodriguez. The Palo Alto P.D. appreciates your cooperation," Tanya said quickly glancing through the file before she placed it on his desk. Tanya reached for her cell phone and speed-dialed Joe Bowman.

"Joe, this is Tanya. Would you please run a check on the name and social security number for one Manuel Garcia?" she asked.

"Did you get everything you need detective?" he asked. "I need to get back to work if you don't mind," he said.

"One more question Jorge. Did Mr. Garcia pick up his last check?" I asked.

"No, I delivered it to him," he said.

"That's weird. Why would you deliver his check to him?" I asked.

"I did it as a favor. I felt sorry for him. He said he was pretty upset and didn't want to return to the golf course," Mr. Rodriguez said.

"Not even to get his check from you?" I asked.

"Did you deliver the check to his house?"

"To this address on his application?" Tanya asked as she copied the address in her notebook.

"Yes, that's the one," he said.

"Here's my card Mr. Rodriguez. Call me if you have anything else for me," Tanya said placing her card on his desk next to the open file.

"Thank you, Jorge," I said as we left. Jorge was already on the phone before we got to the car. He was either calling his boss Mr. Clark, or he was calling Mr. Garcia.

"What do you think Tanya?" I asked.

"He's lying about something," she said.

"Let's go take a look and see where Mr. Garcia lives," I said as we made our way over to the 101.

"You know we would make a good team Tanya," I said.

"That's funny, I was thinking the same thing," Tanya said.

"Get out of here."

"Just for a minute," she said smiling.

It didn't take long to find his house.

"Hey, this is a delightful place. Mr. Garcia owns a shopping mall. Mr. Garcia's address is for a mailbox store location," I said as we pulled up to the storefront.

"Do you want to go inside Harry?"

"Do we need to?"

"Let's go inside anyway and see how long Mr. Garcia has been using this address," Tanya said.

The owner was very cooperative and told us, "Mr. Garcia has only been in here twice since he opened an account at her store.

"That's all?" I asked.

"Yes, the first time was when he signed up and just the day before yesterday," she said.

"Did a short heavyset Hispanic guy come in here the other day with an envelope for Mr. Garcia?" I asked.

"Yes, some guy did come in. We usually don't take packages or mail from someone. Only items that are mailed. However, he explained that it was for one of his employees and he needed to get his last paycheck to him," she said.

"So, he came and got it?" Tanya asked.

"He sure did. And he had a package for me to give to the guy who dropped off his envelope also," she said.

"Did you get his name?" Tanya asked.

"Jorge Rodriguez," she said.

"Did you see him?" I asked.

"Yes, I was working yesterday, and he came in," she said.

"One more thing, Mr. Garcia closed his account."

"Did he leave a forwarding address?" I asked.

"No, he didn't."

"Thank you, ma'am," Tanya said as we left the store.

"Do you want to go back and arrest Jorge?" I asked.

"No, let's make him sweat for a little while," she said.

Just as we were getting into the car, Tanya got a call from Joe Bowman.

"Oh, hi Joe, what did you find out?" she asked, turning to me. "The social checks out for Manuel Garcia all right. Unfortunately, Manuel Garcia has been dead for ten years," she said.

"Are you sure?" I asked.

Tanya waved at me to be quiet, still listening to what Detective Bowman had to say.

"That's okay Joe, thanks for the help," she said pushing the button on her cell phone and ending the call.

"Now, what do you want to do?" I asked.

"Looks like Mr. Rodriguez is not cooperating with us like he should. I wonder if there is anything else he is hiding from us?" Tanya asked.

"If you ask me, I bet he's involved with Garcia somehow," I said.

"It's obvious he's up to something, but what? Why would Rodriguez go to the extreme of delivering Garcia's paycheck to a mailbox store? Why wouldn't Garcia just go to the golf course and pick it up?" she asked.

"Let me ask you this? If you murdered someone, would you want to go back to the murder scene?"

169

"Probably not," Tanya said.

"It still doesn't make sense to what the tie-in is with Garcia and Rodriguez. Rodriguez has to be hiding something, but what?" I asked.

"Hey, didn't that lady at the mailbox store say she gave Rodriguez an envelope?" Tanya asked.

"She sure did," I said.

"Garcia is paying off Rodriguez to be quiet!" we both said together.

"We should go back and get him right now. Rodriquez isn't going anywhere," she said.

"Do you want to go have a late lunch?" I asked.

"No, I need to go back to the office. But you can invite me to have an early dinner with you. How does that sound?" she asked.

"That's great. How about I pick you up around 5:30?"

"No, I'll meet you at the Rusty Scupper," she said.

"That works for me."

Tanya brought me back to the station. I was tired and I decided I would head back to Long Ball's and take a nap. I almost fell asleep a couple of times on the bike. When I got back to Long Ball's house he wasn't there. The place was quiet and perfect for me to take a nice two-and-a-half-hour nap. I went over in my mind about all the things that happened today. What is Jorge up to? What is his connection with Garcia? And the last thing I remembered was how beautiful Tanya looked. I wanted her back and drifted off to sleep.

I felt refreshed and ready to go. It was a little after five when I arrived at the restaurant. It was a short twenty-minute ride for me. I sat at the bar nursing a beer waiting for Tanya to show up. The restaurant and bar shared the same nautical theme throughout the place. Portholes for windows, fishing paraphernalia, rowboats, and anchors bolted to the walls. I was just about halfway through with my beer when I noticed Tanya at the hostess stand. My goodness, she is a goddess. The hostess must have told her that I was in the bar waiting for her because she pointed her in the right direction to find me. I couldn't believe what I was seeing before me. Tanya wore this beautiful red dress that went slightly below her right knee and then angled down a little further below her left knee. The dress seemed to flow with her every step she took towards me. And of course, all the accessories matched perfectly; including the red spaghetti-strapped red heels and red handbag. I'm glad I decided to wear my blue blazer, blue mock turtleneck sweater, and gray slacks instead of my jeans I said to myself.

"Hello Harry," she said in a sultry voice.

"Hello Tanya, you look absolutely stunning this evening," I said standing up and hugging her.

"Can I get you a drink?" I asked sliding her chair back for her to be seated.

"I'll have an iced tea," she said to the bartender as he came over to us.

"How about you sir?" he asked.

"I'm fine thank you," I said.

A waiter dressed in black slacks with a white apron, a white-sleeved dress shirt, and a black tie came up to us and said, "Mr. and Mrs. Clancy, your table is ready.

We looked at each other and started laughing.

"Did I say something wrong?" the waiter asked.

"No, not at all," I said. "It's just that we are not married," I said to him.

"Well, you should be, you make a stunning couple," he said as he led us over to our table.

"What about the drink that we ordered?" I asked.

"Not to worry, I'll bring it over to you," he said heading back to the bar.

"So, what do you think Mrs. Clancy?"

"I think this is rather nice Mr. Clancy," she said smiling.

"Here's your drink ma'am," our waiter said as he placed a napkin down before he placed her glass on the table.

"My name is Martin, and I will be your waiter this evening. Tonight's specials are Blackened Salmon with a spicy Cajun lemon

172

butter sauce served with dirty rice. We also have Seafood Gumbo, Catfish, or a 16-ounce Prime Rib steak, served with a baked potato and all the fixings," Martin said.

"That sounds wonderful," Tanya said.

"Do you want a few minutes to think it over?" Martin asked. "Can I bring you a bottle of wine? How about a nice Merlot?" the waiter asked.

"That works for me. How about you Tanya?"

"That's fine," she said.

"Give us a few minutes to see if there is anything else on the menu we might want to have," I said.

Martin left and we both picked up our menus pretending to look at them while sneaking glances at each other. I felt that something magical might happen tonight to me.

"Harry, do you want some stuffed mushrooms?"

"Sure, that sounds good. When I saw the mushrooms on the menu, I figured you would order them. Almost every time we went out to dinner when we were dating, you would always order stuffed mushrooms with crab," I said.

"I didn't order them all the time, did I?" she asked laughing.

"Yes, you did. Should we order two?"

"No, one order is fine," she said.

173

"What are you going to get Harry? I know, you'll get the Blackened Salmon," she said.

"Remember that time you tried to make it for me in my apartment? You set off the smoke alarm."

"Don't remind me. Didn't your neighbor call the fire department when she heard the smoke alarm go off?" Tanya asked.

"The fire department got there so quickly. I told the fire chief that there was no fire; just my girlfriend trying to make blackened salmon for me. I told him that she set off the smoke alarm."

"The fire chief saved the salmon for you too. He peeked outside and saw your gas grill. He told me to take the iron skillet with the fish and cook it on the grill instead. He said the smoke wouldn't cause any problems outside. Then, I asked him, how cooking it on the grill would work better for me. He went on to explain that, as firemen, we all have to learn to cook and try different recipes on each other all the time. He said his specialty was Cajun cooking," Tanya said smiling at me.

"It took me two weeks to get the smell of fish out of my apartment," I said remembering how much fun we had that night.

Martin came back over to our table with some warm bread, water, and wine. He filled our glasses after I nodded my approval, and asked us, "Are you two ready to order?"

"Martin, I'm going to have the Blackened Salmon and Tanya will have the Prime Rib, blackened as well," I said.

"Excellent choice. May I suggest the spinach salad with the hot bacon vinaigrette dressing topped with blue cheese?" Martin asked.

"That sounds great," I said.

"Don't forget the mushrooms," Tanya said.

Martin left to place our order. The soft shadow from the candle on the table cast an elegant glow on Tanya's face. I raised a glass to make a simple toast, "To us, may we have a new beginning," I said.

"To a new beginning," Tanya said smiling at me with those doe-like brown eyes.

"Give me your hands," she said.

"You're not going to read my palms, are you?" I asked.

"Not at all," she said as she prayed over our food. "Dear Lord please bless this food which we are about to receive and that it be free from any sickness and disease in Jesus' name, Amen."

"Amen," I said.

We didn't let go when we stopped praying. We just held on to the moment.

"Harry, what did you mean about reading your palms?"

"I was joking. When Long Ball and I went to play Pebble Beach the other day, we met our caddy's wife, Maria O'Brien. Mrs. O'Brien told

175

me she was a psychic and could tell a lot by people's hands. The caddy is a friend of Long Ball's," I said.

"What did she tell you?"

"Mrs. O'Brien said that she is a beautiful woman. You must let go of the pain and hurt that she caused you so you can move on. And, that I need to forgive you," I said.

"Do you forgive me, Harry?"

"Of course, I do, I just want to know why you left me like that at the altar?"

"Harry, I wish I could tell you right now, but I can't. Trust me, I will eventually. Harry, I am so happy to see you again. You've always held a special place in my heart," Tanya said.

Martin came over with our salads, which caused a momentary break from our union. As soon as he left, we rejoined our hands again. I thought to myself; what is she hiding, as I looked at her trying to figure it out.

Our main course arrived, and Martin was surprised that we hadn't touched our salads yet. Our hands were still entwined. When we did release to enjoy our meal, we knew that the magic was back. It never left. It was just hidden.

We drank more wine and began to flirt with one another. We were laughing throughout our meal. After dessert, we went outside into the cool moonlit night and strolled along the walkway of the marina holding hands.

"Tanya, I've enjoyed being with you this evening. It's almost like we have never been apart," I said as I pulled her closer to me to embrace her in my arms.

"I know Harry. I've missed you so much. I'm reminded of you every day," Tanya said resting her head against my chest.

I held onto Tanya longing to kiss her. As our lips got closer, neither one of us wanted this moment to end. That's when the chirp of Tanya's cell phone changed the atmosphere between us. As I let go of her, she faded away. It was as if I was waking up from a dream. A dream, I'm wishing for it not to end as she answered the phone.

"Hello, this is Detective Jones," she said. "It's Joe Bowman," she said putting her hand over the phone. "He's what!" Tanya shouted. "Okay, I'm on my way. I'll be there in thirty minutes, thanks, Joe."

"What's up, Tanya?"

"Jorge Rodriguez is dead. Maybe we should have gone back like you suggested Harry," Tanya said.

"How?"

"Joe didn't give me all the details. But I need to go over there and cut our date short," she said.

"I understand. Can I go over there with you?" I asked.

"No, I prefer if you stayed away and let me handle it. I will fill you in. I'll see you at the funeral tomorrow," she said.

"Come on! There is no reason that I shouldn't be able to go over there, Tanya. I thought we were working on this together, we are, aren't we?"

"Harry, please stay away."

"Okay fine," I said as I walked her over to her car.

I waited a few minutes before I left. Tanya didn't tell me where they found Jorge Rodriguez's body, but I assumed it was over at the golf course. When I arrived at the golf course there were several squad cars with red and blue lights flashing. The area surrounding the maintenance building was marked off with yellow crime scene tape. The Crime Scene Investigation Unit was there, collecting any shred of evidence they could find. It wasn't long before Tanya spotted me. The look on her face was not the joyous one who was ready to kiss me at the marina walkway earlier this evening. It was more like, what the hell are you doing here? I told you not to follow me here type of look.

I tried to get a closer look when I heard Tanya yell, "Officer, would you please escort that gentleman over there in the blue blazer to get off the property immediately? His name is Harry Clancy!"

"I'm sorry Mr. Clancy, you need to leave the premises right now sir," the officer said grabbing my right elbow to escort me.

"Excuse me, officer, you better let go of me before I hurt you," I said slipping out of his grasp and running over towards Tanya. Two other cops tackled me just before I made it to the crime scene tape. Tanya glanced over at me again with a disgusted look on her face and said to the officers, "I thought I told you to get him out of here."

"Yes ma'am," the officers said in unison as they escorted me to my motorcycle.

I was furious and decided I better head back to Long Ball's house. Tomorrow was going to be a rough day for everyone.

CHAPTER NINE

UNCOMFORTABLE SILENCE

Nine black limos are lined up in front of Tommy and Brenda Jackson's home waiting to be filled with grieving family members. As far as funerals go, it wasn't a gloomy gray day, but a spectacular sunny day with a cloudless blue sky. A nice cool comforting breeze gently blew from the Pacific. Relatives in all shapes and sizes came out of the house dressed in black. Some were young, some old, some in tears, and others trying to laugh as if it was a normal day for them. Tommy, like his wife, was in tears, both struggling down the walkway to the first limousine. Long Ball and I trailed behind them. The limos snaked along the predetermined route to the church as the motorcycle escorts blocked the intersections to allow us to move freely on the roadways. Tommy and Brenda sat quietly remembering moments they shared with Nina. Only their sobs would interrupt the uncomfortable silence as we drove on. People were on the steps of the church when we arrived.

They were milling around waiting for the service to begin with our arrival. The white hearse parked out front was empty. Nina was inside.

One of the funeral directors came over to Tommy and Brenda as we were getting out of the limo and told them how the procession would be assembled. "Please everyone, I need you to line up after the Jacksons in the order of the limousine you came in," he said.

"How are you doing my friend?" I asked Long Ball as I took a deep breath buttoning up my suit jacket.

"I'm okay Clancy, I guess. You know how I hate funerals; especially this one," Long Ball said. "Why didn't you make the viewing last night?"

"I couldn't, I was with Tanya."

"Did you get lucky?"

"Yes, I did."

Long Ball had a shocked look on his face, not believing what I said.

"Are you serious?"

"Yes, I am. If you want to say that I was lucky enough to have dinner with her, talk to her, hold her in my arms, and almost kiss her before she got a call to investigate a murder. Yes, then I was lucky all right."

"Who got whacked?" Long Ball asked.

"Jorge Rodriguez, the superintendent at Wild Creek," I said whispering not wanting to draw any attention to our conversation.

"Okay everyone, let's begin," the funeral director said.

The procession began and marched inside the Holy Cross Baptist Church. People stared at us as we walked in as if waiting to see how we would react. They wanted to see if we were going to cry out in sorrow and pain or collapse on the spot. This was a multicultural crowd that came to say their final farewell to Nina Jackson.

As we made our way closer to the front where Nina lay in the open casket, I heard the sobbing get louder from Tommy and Brenda, even Long Ball started crying. I did too as I saw her. A wreath from Pinewood was on a stand next to her casket. I looked around and saw a small contingent from Pinewood including my assistant, Wade Miller. But what disturbed me was to see Leonard Ellis at the funeral. Not only was it strange to see him here at the service. Leonard wasn't sitting with the group from Pinewood. Instead, he's sitting with Mr. and Mrs. O'Brien and their daughter Sarah. It looked as if they had known each other for some time by the way they were conversing.

I looked over at Wade pointing over to where Leonard was sitting. He seemed just as surprised as I was to see Leonard sitting with them. I glanced around to see if Tanya had made it yet, but there was no sign of her. I didn't know if I should try to save a place for her. Nina looked so peaceful as I made my way past her and sat down. The funeral director came over to Nina's casket and closed it for the last time.

The service began with an opening by the pastor telling us what to expect when it is our turn to die.

"This is the one thing that we all have in common with Nina. We are all going to share this fate. It is something we can't hide from or run from. It is going to happen to all of us. We also have a choice of where we want to go. Do we want to take our chances and not believe that there is a heaven or a hell? Or do we want eternal life? The choice is ours," he said.

"Tommy and Brenda, you can rest assured that your daughter is in heaven right now giving praises to our heavenly Father. There is no need to worry about her because she is in a far better place than we are right now. Even though she left us, way too soon. She is safely in His arms, with a new body, not lacking for anything, and in no pain," the pastor said.

The congregation was moved by what the pastor said. People were saying amen and hallelujah as he spoke those words.

The pastor welcomed people to come and say some special words about the time they had with Nina. Several people came up to the pulpit and mentioned how wonderful Nina was, "She was a ray of sunshine, and brought joy to the ones she touched," one of her teachers from high school said. A woman came up and sang,

Amazing Grace, which was one of Nina's favorites.

Towards, the end of the service the pastor gave an altar call to see if anyone wanted to give their life to Jesus, "With every head bowed and every eye closed, is there anyone that would like to give their life to Jesus Christ and have your sins forgiven, please raise your hand."

To my surprise, several people raised their hands. I felt something tugging at me to raise my hand, but I don't think I'm ready yet, or if I ever will be, I told myself. I needed to get my life ready first before I made that type of commitment. Look at what I would have to give up. It was good for those people but not for me right now.

Oh, my God, I don't believe it. "Long Ball, what are you doing?" I asked as I saw him raise his hand. "Are you crazy?" I asked, trying to pull his arm down.

"Let go of me Clancy," he said with tears running down his face. "I need to do this Clancy. I need to get my life straight with God," he said. "If you're smart, you might want to give this a try yourself," Long Ball said.

I sat there stunned in disbelief. Did I just lose my best friend?

"Those of you who committed to follow Jesus, please come forward. There are some people here who have some information to give you and a Bible. On behalf of the staff and myself here at Holy Cross Baptist Church, we want to thank you for making a life-changing decision today. Even in death, God can still use you to make a difference in someone's life. Look at the harvest that Nina's life brought forth. Amen," the pastor said.

I went outside with Tommy and Brenda and waited for Long Ball to come out. I caught up with Wade and asked him, "What's up with Leonard? Did you know he was going to be here?"

"Clancy, I had no idea he was coming to the funeral," Wade said.

"What do you make of the O'Brien's being so chummy with Leonard?"

"I don't know Clancy. I think we better keep a close eye on them. Something doesn't seem right."

"I know what you mean Wade. I can understand sitting with someone and having a conversation. It seems like this isn't the first time that they've spoken to one another. Wade, keep a close eye on Leonard, will you?"

"Sure Clancy, no problem," said Wade.

"Hey Wade, how are you doing?" Long Ball asked as he came over to see us.

"Pretty good, considering the circumstances," Wade said.

"Are you a holy roller now?" I asked.

"Be easy on me Clancy. I don't know what came over me, but I felt compelled to raise my

185

hand. You know, I have felt that something's been missing in my life for quite some time. There was a void. But I feel different somehow. I've been lonely for a long time. I want to tell you something, Clancy. A lot of times, when I'm alone in my hotel room, when I'm on the tour, I would read the Bible that the hotel keeps in the drawer. This wasn't a spur-of-the-moment decision I made today. It has been a confirmation of something that's been gnawing at me for a while. Don't worry, I'm still your friend," he said with sincerity.

"That's reassuring," I said.

"Come on let's go. It's time to head to the cemetery," Long Ball said.

As we pulled into the cemetery and parked near the gravesite, I saw a green canopy over the final resting place for Nina. Long Ball pulled me aside.

"Clancy, this is why I made a choice today. There has to be more to life than just this," Long Ball said to me.

"I know Long Ball. That's why I hate funerals. Don't get philosophical on me right now. I can't handle it," I said.

"That's what I'm trying to tell you, Clancy," he said as we made our way over to where everyone was gathered around Nina.

I listened to the pastor as he read a passage from the Bible and said something about, "Ashes to ashes and dust to dust."

I glanced around trying to see if Tanya made it. A dark blue car crept up slowly searching for a place to park among the other cars. I could tell that it was an unmarked police car. I saw Tanya and her partner Joe Bowman get out and make their way over to us. Even though I'm upset, I'm trying to keep my cool until I get a chance to talk with Tanya. After the pastor said his final words for Nina, everyone headed over to Tommy and Brenda's house for the repast.

I went over to speak with Tanya. Before I could even get a word out Tanya said, "Clancy, you had no business being at the murder scene! This is my jurisdiction and not yours!"

"Hey, I thought we were working on this together. What made you change on me so quickly?" I asked.

Tanya didn't give me a chance to respond. What's up with that? I asked myself.

"Clancy, I don't want to see you. Please don't come by the station. It's off-limits to you. Do you understand?"

"Tanya, this doesn't make a lick of sense to me. What did I do?" I asked as she walked off with her partner back to their car. Long Ball was close enough to hear us and he saw the commotion.

"What did you say to her that got her so upset Clancy?" Long Ball asked.

"Let me go talk to her and see what's up," he said.

"By all means, I like to find out too," I said.

Long Ball got to her just before she got into the car. Tanya stepped away from the vehicle to talk to Long Ball in private. I guess she did that so Jim would not hear what they were discussing. It looked pretty intense to me. Tanya hugged Long Ball and kissed him on the cheek before she got in on the driver's side and drove off with Joe Bowman.

Long Ball came back over to talk to me and tried to explain what got her so riled up.

"Look Clancy, Tanya was upset that you went to Wild Creek. You distracted her from doing her work. Tanya said that she had a wonderful time with you last night and that she let her guard down. She felt vulnerable with you," he said.

"That's it?" I asked.

"Deep down, I think she still loves you, Clancy," he said.

"Do you think so Long Ball?" I asked.

"I think she does, but I think she's hiding something else, or she's not ready to tell you yet," Long Ball said.

"Man, Long Ball, I can't believe it. I've been trying to get a kiss from her ever since I saw her. You walk up to her, and she plants one on your cheek," I said.

"It was nice too."

"Stop it," I said.

"Clancy, Tanya gave me a hug and kiss after I told her what happened at the service. I told her I responded to the altar call. Tanya said she wished she could have been there to see me. Tanya was thrilled that I accepted Jesus Christ as my Lord and Savior."

"So, are you a Jesus freak now?" I asked.

"Clancy, all I know is that I'm making a change in my life, and I needed to do this today. I feel like a weight has been lifted off my shoulders, Clancy. It's like I'm free."

Back at Tommy and Brenda's house people were bringing food and drinks with them. It was like an assembly line in the kitchen. Women took the food and either put it in the refrigerator or placed it on the stove to be heated up. Drinks were stashed in the ice chests and the refrigerator in the garage. Extra tables and chairs were brought in by a rental company and were set up outside on the deck to handle the overflow. One of Brenda's sisters came over and motioned for us to be seated in the dining room. The same women who were working the assembly line in the kitchen brought out plates of food for us. Each plate had fried chicken, ribs, greens, mashed potatoes, and gravy on it.

I tried to mingle with a crowd of relatives from Atlanta, but I couldn't find myself to do so. Under normal circumstances, I would have made a play for this fine lady who was trying to hit on me. I didn't make a move. I'm still concerned about Tanya's reaction. It's like she jilted me all over again.

Long Ball and Wade came over to me trying to cheer me up. Wade had a bottle of Jack Daniels with him and handed it to me. I took a swig straight from the bottle.

"It's my fault Clancy. You're upset with me for inviting Tanya to dinner the other night, aren't you?" Long Ball asked.

"That's part of it," I said taking another swig of Jack Daniels.

"Go easy on that Clancy," Long Ball said.

"I told you I didn't want to see her, but you made sure that I did," I said. "Hey, this stuff is going down real nice," I said stumbling over against the wall and knocking a vase off the table onto the floor shattering it into tiny pieces.

"I'm sorry, Clancy's had a little too much to drink," Wade said to the crowd of people looking at Clancy. "What are you doing Clancy, you, stupid idiot? You better get control of yourself," Wade said grabbing my arm.

"Let go of me, Wade!" I shouted as Wade and Long Ball escorted me outside.

"Go to hell Wade," I said.

I awoke the next morning in the back seat of Long Ball's car rubbing my sore jaw. The last thing I remember was seeing Wade's fist just after I told him to go to hell. Wade and Long Ball must have carried me out to his car and put me in here to sleep it off. I do remember I was getting too loud and obnoxious.

Boy, my head is killing me. I looked at my watch and it was 7:30 in the morning. I saw Tommy coming outside to pick up the morning paper as I crawled out of the backseat of the car.

"Tommy, please accept my apology. I'm sorry about my behavior last night," I said.

"That's okay, Long Ball filled me in," Tommy said.

"It's just that it was awkward seeing Tanya the other night at your home. I didn't expect seeing her would make me feel this way. Let alone getting my emotions all stirred up again and going out to dinner with her. I let my guard down," I said.

Tommy invited me in for some coffee and something to eat. We were the only ones up. Everyone else was still sleeping.

Tommy poured me a cup of coffee and brought it over to the kitchen table along with a bottle of Advil. He went over to the automatic dispenser in the refrigerator door and filled a glass of water for me.

"Thanks, Tommy," I said flipping the cap off the bottle of Advil and shaking out four tablets.

Brenda came into the kitchen and hugged her husband.

"Sorry about the vase," I said.

"It's okay Clancy. The vase was from the Ming Dynasty," she said smiling.

Other relatives moseyed into the kitchen looking for a cup of coffee and for something to eat. Everyone seemed to be thinking of Nina; realizing that this was the first day she would be gone forever. Tommy started to well up.

"This reminds me of the times we would go up to Lake Tahoe for Christmas and go skiing," Tommy said pouring pancake batter onto a hot griddle.

"Nina loved going to Lake Tahoe for Christmas, unfortunately, she won't be with us this year or ever again," Tommy said as Brenda came over to wipe the tears away from her husband's face.

It hurts to see everyone so shaken up. I can't imagine what it feels like to lose a child. Parents are supposed to go before their children. It just isn't right for the parents to outlive their kids. It is especially hard to lose someone like Nina. She had so much to offer. No telling how well she would have done on the LPGA Tour.

"Clancy, you have to find her killer," Tommy pleaded with me.

"Tommy, you have my word on it. Even if it means working with Tanya," I said reassuringly to Tommy.

CHAPTER TEN

PICTURES FOR A THOUSAND

After breakfast, I headed back to Long Ball's place. The coffee and the Advil kicked in enough to help me steady myself on Long Ball's Harley. This is such a nice motorcycle that I might consider getting one of these when I get back home. Long Ball said he had some errands to run before we headed back up to Spokane. That's good because I wanted to talk to Nina's and Sarah's golf coach at Stanford before we leave this afternoon.

The extra-long hot shower energized me back into a normal functioning individual. I grabbed a towel off the hook when the doorbell rang. I opened the door a crack and peeked around to see who it was. "Wade, what are you doing here?" I asked.

"Clancy, there's something I should let you know. I wanted to tell you last night, but you were in no shape to hear what I had to say. I followed Leonard and the O'Brien's after the service yesterday as you told me. They did go to the cemetery but quickly left. Leonard met the O'Brien's at the Park-Inn Tavern," Wade said.

"Did you go inside?" I asked.

'No way. They would know that I was following them. I just stayed in the car waiting for them to come out," he said.

"How long were they inside?" I asked.

"About an hour," he said.

"Did you see anything unusual?" I asked.

"Do you mean like their daughter kissing some girl outside after her parents left with Leonard," he said.

"You're kidding?" I asked.

"No, I'm not Clancy."

"That sure puts a different spin on things," I said.

"Wade, do you remember what the girl Sarah kissed looked like?"

"Oh yeah, she was Asian. Cute too."

"It must be Lucy," I said.

"Why didn't you follow the O'Brien's?" I asked.

"I figured that Sarah would lead me back to her parents and Leonard."

"Did she?"

"Absolutely, but it gets better. I followed Sarah to some cheap dive motel off Buckeye Avenue. Here's the address," Wade said after handing me a piece of paper with the address on it. "Guess who shows up at the motel?" Wade asked.

"I don't want to know."

"Oh yes you do, Pete Williams."

"He must have come down for the funeral," I said.

"Did you see him there?" Wade asked. "I didn't."

"Come to think of it, neither did I. He was nowhere around. Not at the funeral nor the cemetery," I said.

"Did you take any pictures, Wade?"

"Of course, I did. Do you think I'm that stupid? Give me some credit Clancy," Wade said handing me an envelope from a one-hour photo shop.

"Take a look at these Clancy. The pictures show all of them together at the motel: Leonard, Sarah, Maria, Peter, and Johnny. I even got one with Sarah kissing that one girl."

"It doesn't make sense Wade," I said flipping through the pictures. "Sure enough, that's Lucy kissing Sarah."

"Are you going to tell Long Ball?" asked Wade.

"Not yet," I said. "But I think I'm going to tell Theresa what's going on."

"Who's Theresa?"

"Theresa is Lucy's girlfriend," I said. "She's cute too. Theresa works for the Palo Alto P.D. Theresa's got an administrative job working behind the information desk," I said.

"What's she got to do with all this Clancy?"

"I'm not sure yet, but I think it's going to stir up the pot Wade."

"Okay," Wade said, not sure how to take it.

"Listen, I met Officer Blake, Theresa, at the police station when I went to go see Tanya. Theresa was there and we talked. Theresa invited me to go to the Park-Inn for drinks."

"Did you go?"

"Yeah, I went with her. That's where her girlfriend Lucy showed up. Lucy owns the Park-Inn Tavern. It's a lesbian bar."

"I gathered that Clancy."

"Do you think Sarah's parents know that their daughter is gay or bisexual?" I asked.

"I'm not sure they know Clancy. Why would they meet at a gay bar?' Wade asked. "That to me should be a tip-off for the O'Brien's that their daughter likes it that way," he said.

"Wade, do me a favor, will you?" Go back to the motel and ask for Leonard's room. See if he is still there."

"No problem."

"I'm going to see Theresa at the police station first and then talk to the golf coach at Stanford," I said closing the door as he walked out to leave.

I went back upstairs to get dressed. I put on a pair of jeans, a white polo shirt, and my tennis shoes. I felt like I was forgetting something as I went outside to the garage. My light jacket was still on the bike where I left it earlier this morning. Then it hit me, my gun. My Beretta was still inside the gun case in my bag. I wanted to make sure I had it with me just in case. The Road King has these locking hard-shell case saddle bags. My gun should be safe inside them. The last thing I need to do is walk into the police station with a loaded weapon. A big no-no; and Black too. I don't think so.

I wanted to make sure that Tanya was gone. I didn't want to run into her at the police station. Luckily, Theresa was on duty and answered the phone.

"Hey Theresa, this is Harry Clancy. Is Tanya working today?" I asked.

"Hello Clancy, good to hear your voice. What can I do for you?" she asked. "Yeah, Tanya's working today. She's not in right now. Tanya is out on a call with Detective Bowman. I saw them leave about twenty minutes ago," she said.

"Theresa, she's not the one I want to see, it's you."

"Why Clancy, I never knew. I don't go both ways. You know my persuasion, Mr. Clancy," Theresa said.

"I know, I have something I need to show you. Can I meet you somewhere?" I asked.

"It's too bad you're not here. I have a fifteen-minute break in five minutes," she said.

197

"Great, meet me at the fountain out front," I said.

"Where are you, Mr. Clancy?"

"I'm in the parking lot."

"Okay, I'll see you in a few," she said.

Boy, another beautiful day in sunny California. This weather is gorgeous, I said to myself as I walked over to the fountain. If the weather is like this all the time, I could live down here someday.

The fountain was in the middle of a circular memorial for officers killed in the line of duty. I took a glance at the names and saw Officer Lawrence T. Blake. I wonder if that is Theresa's father. I guess I'll find out soon enough.

"Hello Officer Blake, thanks for meeting me on such short notice," I said. "Can I ask you a quick question?"

"Sure, go right ahead," Theresa said.

"Is this your dad's name listed here?"

"Yes, it is."

"I'm sorry, I didn't know."

"Mr. Clancy, when you said you wanted to meet me at the fountain, I just froze. It's hard for me to come over here."

"Believe me, I understand."

"How could you?" she asked.

"My father was a cop too. He was killed while in the line of duty as well. That's what made me decide to be a cop."

"Me too, Mr. Clancy."

I could tell she was upset coming over to see me. I don't know how she's going to react when I show her these pictures.

"What did you want to talk about Mr. Clancy?" she asked.

"Yesterday at Nina's funeral, some people were sitting and talking together that didn't make sense. And I'm trying to make the connection of what all these people have in common. I have some photographs of these people together and I want to see if you can help me figure out what is going on here," I said handing Theresa the envelope with the pictures.

I have the pictures in the order I want Theresa to see them. Starting with Mr. and Mrs. O'Brien and Leonard in church. I don't know how Wade was able to take that picture. Wade must have used his cell phone camera for that one, very inconspicuous. Then, I had one picture at the Park-Inn Tavern. Then the one at the motel and back again to the Park-Inn. Theresa saw the picture of Sarah out front of the Park-Inn by herself. Then she saw the one with Sarah kissing Lucy. Theresa dropped the pictures on the ground and started breathing heavily, almost hyperventilating. She got up and she started going off on me.

"Is this some sort of joke Clancy? Why are you spying on Lucy?" What the hell is going on here?" she asked.

199

"Believe me, Theresa, that was not my intent. I had no idea that Lucy would be involved with Sarah. My partner was following the O'Brien's and this guy," I said pointing to Leonard's picture. "Do you know Sarah O'Brien?" I asked.

"Yeah, she comes in all the time. She's a regular at the Park-Inn."

"Did you suspect that she had a thing for Lucy?" I asked.

"No, not at all."

"So, you say that Sarah is a regular at the bar?"

"Yeah, I know she comes in here at least two or three times a week."

"Do you ever talk to her?"

"Just in passing. I've never had a major conversation with her," she said with her eyes welling up. "I can't believe that Lucy would do that to me. We've been together a long time," she said looking at the other pictures again.

"This guy has been in there before," she said pointing to Pete Williams.

"Are you sure?"

"Oh yeah, he came in with Sarah before. And come to think of it, Sarah and this light-skinned Black girl came in together one time and that guy in the picture," she said.

I took the picture of Nina out of my wallet and showed it to Theresa.

"That's her! That's the girl they came in with!" Theresa yelled.

"That's Nina Jackson, the Stanford coed that was murdered last week. Her uncle and I are very good friends. He hired me to help find out who killed his niece. Nina's uncle, Al Jackson, is a professional golfer on the Senior PGA Tour. I don't know if you know this or not, but Nina was the fourth Black golfer to be murdered in the past several months."

"I had no idea, Mr. Clancy. Do you think they are all related?" Theresa asked.

"That's why Al Jackson hired me to protect him at the U.S. Senior Open next week in Spokane, Washington."

"How can I help you, Mr. Clancy?"

"Do you remember anything unusual when they were at the Park-Inn?" I asked.

"Nina seemed to be uncomfortable with them. It looked like they were trying to get her drunk. Nina sat between Sarah and that guy Pete. Both of them were making passes at Nina. A little while later Nina seemed to let her guard down and allowed them both to kiss her. Nina joined Sarah and Pete on the dance floor. She didn't look as uninhibited as before. From the looks of her changed behavior, I think they slipped her some Ecstasy," Theresa said.

"How can you tell?" I asked.

"Remember, I'm a cop. I'm supposed to observe people. I can tell when someone is high

201

on alcohol or drugs. The Park-Inn gets a lot of people high on Ecstasy all the time. And Nina looked like she was high on Ecstasy."

"Is there anything else you can remember?" I asked her.

"Just that all three of them left together," Theresa said looking at her watch. "Hey, I got to get back inside. My break is over," Theresa said getting up to leave.

"Thanks, Theresa, you've been a great help," I said hugging her.

"Let me know if there is anything else I can help you with," she said holding the door open before she went back inside the station.

"I will Officer Blake."

There's one more stop I need to make before Long Ball, and I leave this afternoon and that's at Stanford.

The people at the administration building at Stanford University were very helpful in telling me where I could find Patty Hill, the women's golf coach. It's been a while since I was on a college campus.

Fortunately, Coach Hill was available and could meet with me. Patty Hill was a former member of the LPGA and amateur champion at Stanford. Several trophies and plaques adorned her office wall. She also had pictures of players and teams throughout the years that she helped coach.

"Thanks for seeing me on such short notice Coach Hill," I said sitting down in one of the two brown leather chairs she had on the other side of her desk.

"What can I do for you Mr. Clancy, is that right?" Coach Hill asked.

"Yes, that's right. It's Harry Clancy," I said. "I have some questions about Nina Jackson's murder."

"And why would I want to give you any information concerning Nina?" she asked.

"I'm a private investigator hired by Nina's uncle to find out who killed her," I said.

"That would be Al Jackson," she said.

"You know him?" I asked.

"Oh, sure I know Al Jackson. He came to all her matches when he was in town. At certain times, it was hard to tell who her coach was because he was with her all the time. I must admit he helped her a lot. Nina was one of the best players I've seen in years," she explained.

"What can you tell me about her roommate, Sarah O'Brien?" I asked.

"Sarah is a good player, but she was no match for Nina. Nina was a natural. Sarah on the other hand had to work extra hard," Coach Hill said.

"Did you suspect any jealousy or anything like that?"

"It was obvious she was jealous. All was not rosy with Sarah and Nina. They fought all the time. Not it public, always in private."

"How did you know this?" I asked.

"Nina confided in me," she said.

"Why would she talk to you and not her parents?"

"Come on Mr. Clancy, there are certain things that go on in a kid's life that you don't want your parents to know anything about."

"Such as?"

"Nina planned on moving out of the apartment she shared with Sarah. Nina couldn't take it anymore, especially when she found her ex-boyfriend in bed with Sarah."

"Who was that?" I asked.

"Some guy named Pete Williams," she said.

I was shocked to find out it was Pete Williams. "Are you sure it was Pete Williams?" I asked. "They broke up a long time ago," I said.

"Yeah, I know they did. But he kept coming down here to see her all the time." Coach Hill said.

"Nina wanted to break it off completely. And when she caught him in bed with Sarah that was it."

"Can I ask you a question, Mr. Clancy?"

"Sure, go right ahead."

"What's your interest in Nina?" she asked. "You seem to be not as objective as someone who would be investigating a murder."

"You see, the thing is, I knew Nina when she was a member of Pinewood's junior golf program while she was growing up in Spokane, I said.

"I didn't know you knew her that well Mr. Clancy."

"So, you can see her death is a little personal with me as well," I told her. I knew about her relationship with Pete Williams. I still don't know what she saw in that guy."

"Coach, what do you make of this?" I asked, showing her a picture of Sarah O'Brien kissing Lucy at the Park-Inn Tavern.

"That's Sarah all right, being the wild one that she is," Coach Hill said.

"I beg your pardon?"

"All I'm saying is Sarah's behavior doesn't surprise me one bit. Sarah is pretty carefree in what she does with her life. However, it disturbed me what she was doing to Nina," Coach Hill said getting up from her desk and looking out the window.

"Such as?" I asked.

"Putting drugs into Nina's Drinks."

"What kind of drugs coach?" I asked, looking more concerned.

"Ecstasy."

"How did you find out?"

"Nina. I told you that she confided in me, didn't I?"

"Yes, you did," I said.

Coach Hill was standing by the window looking out when she started telling me what happened to Nina.

"Nina called me about 4:00 A.M. one morning crying hysterically about being raped by Sarah and Pete. Nina said she just left them at a motel over by the Park-Inn Tavern. Nina said she wanted to come over and talk to me."

"Did you call the cops?"

"No," she said as she started to cry.

"Why not?"

"I couldn't call them."

"What?"

"After Nina came over, I calmed her down and she told me the whole story. Nina didn't know how Ecstasy works. She didn't know she was drugged until it was too late. Mr. Clancy, everything is intensified with that drug, especially, sex."

"What in the world are you saying, Coach Hill?" I asked, picking up her phone ready to call the cops.

"Put the phone down Mr. Clancy, let me explain," she said.

"How would you know?"

"I've taken it before. You see Mr. Clancy; Nina was special to me. But Sarah had control over me. I went to a party that some of the

206

students were having off-campus. Sarah invited me."

"Let me guess. All females?" I asked.

"Yes."

"Is that when you got familiar with Ecstasy?"

"Yeah, Sarah gave me this pill and told me how fantastic it was."

"Was it?"

"It was incredible. I couldn't believe it. I let my inhibitions fall by the wayside of my better judgment Mr. Clancy. Unfortunately, I let them fall too much. Sarah took pictures of me in uncompromising positions."

"Sarah is blackmailing you, isn't she?"

"Yes, she has me over a barrel. I can handle the gay thing. It's the drugs that could get me in trouble. My career and reputation would be ruined if any of this got out," she said.

"Why are you telling me then?" I asked.

"Because I don't care anymore. Not since Nina was killed," she said.

"What else happened that night with Nina?"

"After Nina slept it off, I asked her if she wanted to talk to her parents about it. Under no circumstances did she want to talk to her parents. Nina said it would destroy them. She told me she was a virgin before they raped her."

"That must have been reassuring for you?" I asked. "Very convenient."

"I called Sarah and told her that I was taking care of Nina. I also told her it's over between us."

"Sarah told me I was making a big mistake and threatened to use the photos against me if I said anything to the police."

I noticed a picture on her desk of Coach Hill, two kids, and someone I assumed was her husband. Coach Hill, or is it Mrs. Hill?" I asked as I picked up the picture to look at it more closely.

"It's Mrs. Hill," she said shamefully.

"You're having an affair?"

"Our marriage was on the rocks anyway, so it's no big deal."

"Did he find out?" I asked.

"Yes, he did. We've been separated for six months. The divorce will be final soon."

"What about the kids?" I asked.

"My husband agreed not to say anything if I gave him full custody of the children, which I did."

"You sure got yourself in a mess."

"I'm trying to do my best to get out of it if I still can," she said.

"Anything else happened that morning?" I asked.

"Sarah came over and threatened to kill me if I talked to the authorities. I must admit, I was scared and decided I should keep my mouth shut. But with Nina's death; I don't care anymore. I told Sarah I had a tape of what Nina told me and of your threat."

"Coach Hill, you need to go to the police and let them know what's going on," I said. "Otherwise, you're a dead woman."

Coach Hill's door was ajar as her secretary peeked in, "Is everything okay Coach Hill?"

"Yes Peggy, thank you," Coach Hill said.

"That's what Sarah said. Sarah wanted me to give her the tape. Sarah's supposed to come over to see me later this afternoon," Coach Hill said.

"You're not going to give it to her, are you?" I asked.

"Yes, I am."

"You're crazy! Do you think she's going to let you go after you give her the tape?" I asked.

"Don't worry Mr. Clancy, I made a copy of the tape. It's in a safe deposit box," she said looking like a condemned woman.

"One other question Coach Hill. Where does your team practice?" I asked, getting up from the chair to leave.

"At Wild Creek. The same place where they found Nina's body," she said.

CHAPTER ELEVEN

OVERWHELMING EMOTIONS

I decided that as much as I hated to do it, I had to see Tanya and let her know about my visit with Coach Hill. I didn't want to go inside the police station, so I waited outside for Tanya to show up. I gave Officer Blake a call to see if Tanya had come back yet.

"Yes Mr. Clancy, Tanya is in the office. Do you want me to ring Detective Jones for you?"

"No, that's okay. I will wait for her to come outside since it is so close to noon," I said.

"Goodbye, Mr. Clancy."

"Thank you, Officer Blake," I said hanging up the phone.

Finally, Tanya came out, but she was not alone. Her partner, Detective Joe Bowman was with her. Tanya's heading directly over to me like she's on a mission from God.

"Harry, what are you doing here?" Tanya asked as she looked me straight in the eyes.

"Did Officer Blake tell you I was out here?"

"Yes, she did."

"Tanya, I wanted to talk to you about my visit with Coach Hill."

"Harry, you need to leave. I don't want to hear any of it. Do you understand?" she asked.

Detective Bowman butts in and gets between me and Tanya. I could not believe it; Detective Bowman shoved me and said with his hand in my face, "Mr. Clancy if you know what's good for you, I suggest that you leave."

I have always had a tough time submitting to authority. I immediately felt my right hand forming into a fist and delivering a blow to Detective Bowman's mouth. As quickly as Detective Bowman hit the ground, other officers saw what happened and subdued me. By this time, my face was on the ground looking up at Detective Bowman as Tanya and the other officers were helping him up.

"Clancy, you're in a lot of trouble!" Detective Bowman yelled as the officers took me inside and threw me into a holding cell.

It seemed like it was an hour before anyone came to see me. Fortunately, it was Tanya. She had another officer with her who opened the cell door to let me out.

"Come with me Harry," Tanya said as the officer handcuffed me and escorted me out.

"I have arranged for us to go into a room to talk privately Harry," Tanya said pointing for me to go inside.

"Thanks, Tanya. Can you take these handcuffs off me?" I asked looking at my bloody face in the two-way mirror.

"No, I think I'm going to let you wear them just a little while longer. What were you thinking Harry? Why did you hit my partner? That was a very stupid thing to do," she said.

"How private is this room, Tanya?" I asked, pointing to the mirror.

"Don't flatter yourself, Harry. No one is behind the mirror waiting to hear what you have to say," she said.

"Hey, for what it's worth, I am sorry about your partner. Is he okay?" I asked.

"He'll survive. I'm trying to talk him out of pressing charges against you," she said.

"Like I was trying to tell you earlier, I was over at Stanford visiting with Patty Hill, the women's golf coach. I wanted to see what I could find out about Sarah O'Brien and Nina."

"Well, what did you find out?" Tanya asked.

"Tanya, you're not going to believe what I am about to tell you."

"Try me."

"Coach Hill told me so much stuff that I'm still trying to decipher it all. Sarah was very jealous of Nina and was not happy being the number two player on the team. It was obvious that when Nina got out of school and turned pro, she would be all set with endorsements. You can

212

credit a lot of that to her father with his connections in the advertising business," I said.

"Coach Hill said that Nina and Sarah fought all the time and that Nina confided in her. But the real kicker is Nina's ex-boyfriend, Pete Williams. They both drugged Nina and raped her. They slipped her a dose of Ecstasy and raped her."

"Oh my God, are you kidding me? Why didn't Nina press charges, or for that matter, why didn't Coach Hill call the police?" Tanya asked.

"It gets deeper still. Sarah was blackmailing the coach. It appears that Coach Hill liked it both ways. Coach Hill had an ongoing affair with Sarah O'Brien."

I went on to tell Tanya about the all-girl party that the coach attended, and the intimate pictures Sarah had of Coach Hill. "Sarah threatened to take the pictures to the Dean, which would destroy her career and her marriage if she didn't cooperate with Sarah. Coach Hill went along with it for a while up until Nina's murder. I guess she finally had enough and decided it was time to let the truth out," I explained.

"Why didn't Nina go to her parents?" Tanya asked.

"Nina was a virgin, and she didn't want her parents to find out. It would have destroyed them," I said.

"I can understand that Harry, but this is rape. It should not go unpunished," Tanya said.

213

"That's why I came back here to see you, Tanya. I tried to get the coach to contact the police. Believe me, I was ready to take it out on her. I was really upset with Coach Hill. It still didn't make sense for her not to go to the authorities over this."

"What did you find out with Jorge Rodriguez?" I asked.

"The only clue I have about Jorge Rodriquez's murder is a matchbook with the name 19th Hole on it. Looks like he used it to light the cigar that was still burning in his ashtray when his body was found with his throat slit," Tanya said.

"Tanya, do you have any idea where Stanford's golf team practices?" I asked.

"Don't tell me, Wild Creek? How convenient," Tanya said.

"One more thing Tanya. Coach Hill taped a conversation she had with Nina in her office, which explains the whole setup with Sarah O'Brien and Pete Williams. Coach Hill told Sarah that she had a tape of everything that happened with Nina. Unfortunately, Sarah still has control over Coach Hill. Sarah is going to stop by Coach Hill's office this afternoon to pick up the tape," I said.

"She's just going to give her the tape?" Tanya asked.

"Don't worry Tanya, Coach Hill made a copy of the tape and has it in a safe deposit box in case anything happens," I said.

"Well, that's good."

"Are you going to send someone over there to keep an eye out for Sarah?" I asked.

"Not yet."

"Why not?"

"I want to see if we can get Pete Williams," Tanya said.

"That makes sense," I said. What about me?" I asked.

"Hold tight, I'm going to talk to Joe and see if I can convince him not to press charges against you and get you out of here," Tanya said.

"I'm not going anywhere."

About forty minutes later Tanya met me outside after I was released. Tanya talked to her partner and convinced him not to press charges against me. I don't know how she did it this fast. Thank God, she was able to get me out of here. That boy wanted me dead.

"Thanks, Tanya, I appreciate you doing this for me. It's a miracle that I got out of jail," I said.

"Yes, Harry it certainly is, and you owe me," she said.

We both went over both murders again and tried to piece together what pieces we were missing, "You know Tanya, there is one person we have not spoken to," I said.

"Who's that Harry?"

"The reporter from the television station who interviewed you and Manuel Garcia," I said.

"You know Harry that's right," she said smiling.

Maybe I got a reprieve and I'm off Tanya's condemned list. "Do you want to hop on the Harley and go with me?" I asked. "I have an extra helmet."

Tanya took one look at me as if I was crazy or something, and said, "Harry, what am I wearing?"

"Well, a very nice gray skirt that shows off those gorgeous legs of yours. Which wouldn't look too ladylike on a motorcycle I suppose."

'Duh!" she said.

"I tell you what, why don't I follow you in your car?"

"Brilliant idea Harry, absolutely brilliant," she said teasing me.

"Tanya, do you remember the reporter's name?"

"Julie, Julie Monroe. Yeah, that's it," she said.

"You know Tanya, I owe Julie Monroe a lot," I said.

"Why's that Harry?"

"Well, you see if it wasn't for Julie interviewing you, I never would have seen you. Do you know, everything about us came back to me when I saw you on TV? I was overwhelmed with emotions Tanya. You looked so good, so beautiful that I flashed back on everything we once had between us. I guess I would like to have it back; you know, the magic," I said hoping to get a positive response from her.

"I understand Harry, but that was so long ago. You need to let it go and move on with your life."

"Tanya, believe me. I had buried you a long time ago and I didn't think I would ever dig you back up. That was the last thing I expected to do or wanted to do. Do you understand?"

"Of course, I do. Harry, seeing you hasn't been easy for me either. Every time I look at you, I am reminded of a mistake I made so many years ago. And believe me, I was happy with my life before you came here too. I'm going through the same thing. It hurt me when I left you at the wedding as well, Harry. I know it must have been embarrassing."

"That's an understatement. I was all dressed up with no place to go," I said.

"Come on, let's get a move on. Why don't you follow me, Harry?" she said, changing the subject.

I had never been inside a television station before, and this was a unique experience. There's a TV in the lobby with a commercial playing.

"Have you seen anything like this before Tanya?"

"No, I haven't," she said.

217

"May I help you?" the lady said behind the receptionist's desk who looks like she could be my grandmother.

"Yes, is it possible to see Julie Monroe?" Tanya asked.

"Yes, it is. She's right behind you," the receptionist said pointing behind us.

Sure enough, Julie was there alright, doing the afternoon news.

"Have a seat, the show is just about over, and I'll let Julie know you are here," she said. "I'm sorry, I did not get your names."

"I'm Detective Tanya Jones with the Palo Alto Police Department," she said flashing her badge.

The receptionist didn't bother asking me who I was. She must have thought I was a cop too.

I could faintly hear the receptionist tell Julie that she had some people out in the lobby waiting for her. I thought I heard the receptionist ask Julie if she was in some sort of trouble.

A few moments later Julie Monroe came out to meet with us. Her face looked weird from all the extra makeup she had on.

Hello again Detective Jones. And you are?" she asked, looking at me.

"I'm Harry Clancy, I'm a private investigator," I said as we shook hands.

"Is there somewhere we can talk in private Ms. Monroe?" Tanya asked.

"If you don't mind, I'd like to go outside since it is such a beautiful day and eat my lunch. We have a courtyard on the side of the building that should give us some privacy," she said.

"Julie, they need to sign in and get a visitor's badge before they can go back with you," the receptionist said.

"Thanks, Rosie," Julie said handing us our badges. "Follow me. I just need to stop by the breakroom and get my lunch out of the refrigerator."

Julie was right. There were a couple of empty picnic tables for us to choose from. Julie handed Tanya and me some bottled water that she took from the refrigerator for us.

"Please have a seat," she said sitting down across from us.

"What did Manuel Garcia tell you he was doing when he found Nina's body?" Tanya asked.

"He was changing the pin placements on the greens," Julie said.

"Do you remember anything unusual about him?" Tanya asked.

"No, not all, except I noticed he drove one of those flatbed golf carts used to haul shovels and other stuff," Julie said.

"Perfect to haul a body in," I said.

Tanya looked at me as if expecting my next question.

"Tanya, did forensics check any of the equipment at the golf course or the cart that Mr. Garcia used for work that day?" I asked.

"No, they didn't. We didn't have any reason to do that," Tanya said reluctantly.

"Can I ask you another question, Tanya?" I asked.

"Go right ahead Harry," Tanya said getting irritated with me for putting her on the spot in front of the reporter.

"Did you guys figure out how the body got there?"

"We assumed that Nina was dropped there."

"Was the body dragged to the green?" I asked.

"No Harry, it wasn't. We didn't see any evidence that the body was dragged. The body had to have been carried there," she said. "But the murderer could not have done that by himself, could he?" I asked. "If he didn't have any help, he must have used one of the golf carts that Ms. Monroe mentioned."

"By some chance Ms. Monroe, do you think you could remember the golf cart if we went back to the golf course?" Tanya asked.

"I can do better than that. I told you there was something different about that golf cart. I remember seeing the number 31 on the tailgate of the golf cart as he drove off. The golf cart had a mini-truck bed with the number 31 painted on

220

it and a Marine Semper Fi bumper sticker," she said.

"Tanya, you need to call your partner and have him get forensics over to Wild Creek as soon as possible. Even though it has been over a week since Nina's body was discovered. There may be some traces of DNA evidence still on the golf cart. Blood is so hard to clean up you know," I said.

"That's not a bad idea Harry."

Tanya got on the phone and called her partner and told him to get a search warrant and head over to Wild Creek. She explained to him about the information we got from Julie Monroe.

While Tanya was on the phone with her partner, Detective Joe Bowman. I got a call from Long Ball wanting to know where I was. "Hey Long Ball, how's everything?" I asked.

"Good Clancy. I need you to be back at my place within an hour and ready to go," Long Ball said.

"No problem, I'm already packed. I spent the afternoon with Tanya where I got myself thrown in jail earlier today."

"What?" Long Ball asked.

"Don't worry, I'll fill you in later. Other than that, everything has been just great. I'm over at the TV station. Tanya and I met with Julie Monroe; the reporter who interviewed the greenskeeper the day Nina's body was found. It was a lead we went after that might tie in with

Nina's killer," I said. As soon as I said that Tanya gave me a dirty look suggesting that I shouldn't talk too much about something that might not have any bearing on the case.

"What did Long Ball want Harry?" Tanya asked.

"We're taking off this afternoon and heading up the coast. Long Ball wants me to be at his place in an hour," I said.

"Julie, thank you so much for your help. This may be the break we are looking for," Tanya said getting up to leave.

Julie escorted us back to the lobby where we turned in our visitor badges to Rosie.

"Tanya, please share any information you may get with me, okay?" I asked making our way out to the parking lot and over to her car.

"I promise Harry."

"For what it's worth, Long Ball hired me to protect him and find Nina's killer. I need your help with this Tanya," I said pleading with her.

"I guess this is it, Harry?" Tanya said.

"Goodbye Tanya, it was so nice seeing you," I said trying to kiss her. I hugged her before she got into her car.

"You too Harry," she said closing the door.

I watched her pull out of the parking space and waved at her as she drove off. I wasn't sure, but it looked like she had tears streaming down her face. I got back on the Harley and rode off wondering if this was the last time I would ever see Tanya.

CHAPTER TWELVE

THE SETUP

Long Ball had everything packed in the car and ready to go. I rode the Harley into the garage and made sure I got my Beretta out of the saddlebags before we left.

Later that afternoon Long Ball and I made our way out of the Bay Area up the 101 and eventually over onto Interstate-5 North towards Glen Eden Beach, Oregon. We had a ten-hour drive ahead of us. This gives us plenty of time for us to discuss all the events that transpired over the past several days and get some much-needed sleep, or so I thought.

"So, Clancy, what's been going on with you and Tanya?" Long Ball asked.

"Well Long Ball, today was a special day for me. I spent a few hours in jail for punching out Tanya's partner, Joe Bowman," I said.

"What did you do you idiot to get yourself locked up?"

"Like I said, I decked her partner. He put his hand in my face and shoved me, so I let him have it."

"Are you crazy? I hired you to protect me; not to get yourself thrown in jail."

"You're right, I'm sorry."

"Anything else happened that I should know about?" Long Ball asked.

"Yes, there is. Remember I told you Jorge Rodriguez the superintendent at Wild Creek was found murdered with his throat slit?"

"Where did they find him?"

"They found him in his office at the golf course."

"Do they have any idea who might have killed him?"

"My hunch is that the killer is Manuel Garcia. The same guy who killed Nina."

"Do you have any clues?" Long Ball asked.

"Only one, a matchbook with the 19th Hole written on it," I said. "Long Ball, I think Jorge knew more about Manuel Garcia than he led us to believe. Jorge must have found out something else about Garcia and threatened him with it."

"How was it saying goodbye to Tanya?"

"It was hard."

"Do you think you'll see her again? Or, should I say, do you want to see her again?"

"Most definitely, but I don't think she will want to see me."

"Why do you say that Clancy?"

"You know we talked, but every time it seemed like we were getting closer, something happened to stop the moment."

"Did you kiss her?"

"No, I didn't. Believe me, I tried on several occasions. And she turned me down. That's why I think I probably won't see her."

"Why would you say that? You're tied in with her on the case, aren't you?"

"Yes, I am. I only hope that Tanya is willing to share with me any information she may get."

"Clancy, I'll pray about it," Long Ball said as we pulled into the drive-thru at the Golden Arches.

We went to the gas station across the street from the fast-food joint and filled it up before heading out on the interstate. We still had a long way to go to get onto I-5. Long Ball started talking again about praying, about God, and stuff between bites of his burger.

"Clancy, I know you must be tripping about me getting saved; I've been reading the Bible. I'm getting a lot out of it," Long Ball said taking a sip of his chocolate milkshake.

"Hey Long Ball, I understand how you feel. It's something new and if it works for you, that's great. You go right ahead. I'm not one to criticize you for your beliefs. Just don't try to get me over to your side. Do you understand?"

"Of course, Clancy. I wouldn't do that to you."

"I hope not."

"You know Clancy, it's just like trying to quit smoking. Remember how much you tried to break me of my two-packs-a-day habit?"

"Yeah, it was tough?"

"Well, that's the same way with Christianity. I can't make you become a believer. It's when the time is right for you. I woke up one morning and decided to go for a run. I don't know what came over me; I just decided to go out for a run. Do you know, it was one of the most difficult runs I ever had. I could barely breathe. I felt like I was coughing up a lung, it was so bad. Afterward, I showered and got dressed to go to the driving range to practice. However, the first thing I noticed when I got into my car was my ashtray. It overflowed with cigarette butts and my car reeked of cigarette smoke. I lit one up anyway. It tasted so bad. I put it out after a couple of puffs. From that day forward, I quit smoking cigarettes. That was August 1, 1985. That's the best thing I could have ever done for myself. It saved my life."

"So, what's the link?" I asked.

"Well Clancy, it's like this. God wants you to come to Him when your spirit is broken. You know something is missing in your life. You want more, but you don't know how to get it. I'm not talking about material things. I'm talking

227

about the meaning of your existence here on this planet. You could have talked to me until you were blue in the face about the dangers of smoking. I still wasn't going to stop until I was ready to stop. You'll come around to it when you know it is time. I'm not going to force you, my friend."

"Thank you, I appreciate that," I said.

"My job is to tell you about the good news."

"And what's that?" I asked.

"That Jesus died for you on the cross so that you may live and have life more abundantly."

"I never heard you talk like this Long Ball. I'm happy for you."

"Clancy, it's great, a weight has been lifted off my shoulders. I am free. I am free to be me. I understand.

Clancy, I can only hope that you see God's light shine through me and that He can touch you. You will never be the same again."

"It sounds like a crutch for you Long Ball, but if that works for you, great."

"You know Clancy. If it is a crutch for me, I couldn't ask for a better one than having God there to help heal me of my sins, hurts, sorrows, and dreams that I lost."

"Good for you Long Ball," I said as I drifted off into a deep sleep.

I was jarred out of my sleep when the Maserati hit a pothole. I glanced at the clock on the dashboard; it read 11:57. We are close to Glen Eden. I didn't let Long Ball know I was awake. I kept my eyes closed. I had a terrible nightmare. I dreamt we were in an accident, and I died. Long Ball lost control of the car as it skidded off an embankment and plunged into the river. We were drowning. I saw Long Ball being engulfed by a radiant light and two angels were carrying him up further into the light. All three of them looked at me with sadness in their eyes. But all I could see was the darkness as I was being pulled down into the abyss. I felt pain in my lungs as they were filling up with water and my life was leaving me. I didn't see any angels, but I felt claws digging into my body as I was being dragged deeper into the darkness as the last stream of light vanished from Long Ball. What have I done? I asked myself. I saw a collage of all the evil things I did in my life. The people I killed when I was in the Gulf War, my fornication, and the others that I hurt. I saw all my sins. All I could say was that I'm sorry. I'm so sorry. I heard a voice say, "You have one more chance. Do you want to take it?" Before I could say yes, I was jolted awake by another pothole in the road.

"Wake up Clancy, we're here," Long Ball said parking in front of the office of the Beach Inn.

"Where are we?" I asked.

"At the Beach Inn. My God, what happened to you, Clancy? You look like you saw the devil."

"I did," I said. "I had a terrible dream. We were in a car accident and we both died. You went to heaven, and I went to hell," I said grabbing Long Ball's arm as he was getting out of the car.

"You see, God's trying to tell you something, Clancy. You better listen."

"I know, I heard a voice asking me if I want another chance," I said trembling.

"Do you want to end up where you were going? Why would you want to be in darkness when you can have God's light shine upon you?" Long Ball asked.

"The dream shook me up Long Ball. I will think about what you said."

We arrived just after midnight. Long Ball and I went to the front desk to wake up the manager so we could check in and get our keys. A gruff old man came out to meet us just barely awake.

"You boys are getting in here kind of late, aren't you?" he asked passing the registration book over to Long Ball to fill out.

"Yes sir, we are. We came in from San Jose," I said.

"Hey, you look familiar. Where you from?" he asked looking at Long Ball.

"I'm originally from Spokane. My parents used to take me here every summer when I was a little boy," Long Ball said.

The man looked at the registration book and said, "We used to have some black folks that used to come down here. Their name was Jackson. I was a teenager when they started coming here. Nice folks, Albert, and Winnie Jackson," he said smiling, happy that he was able to remember their names.

"I'm their son, Al Jackson Jr., I remember you. You used to mow the lawn all the time. Your parents had you running around like a Hebrew slave," Long Ball said.

"They sure did," the old man said extending his hand to shake Long Ball's hand. "My name is Sam Morrison. Aren't you some fancy golfer nowadays?" he asked.

"Yes, I am. I play on the Senior PGA Tour."

"Here are your keys. Number 106. The same cottage you and your family used to get. How many nights are you staying?" Sam asked.

"Just two. We're going to play Glen Eden Country Club in the morning," Long Ball said.

"Thank you," I said as we walked outside and over to the car.

Long Ball parked the car in front of our cottage. We brought our bags inside and left the golf clubs in the car. I stayed inside while Long Ball parked the Maserati across the parking lot where there were fewer cars. I guess he is being overly protective of his new car and doesn't want to get any door dings.

"Like I was telling the old man. Our family would come here every summer to dig for clams. I know it's a little rustic, but you'll like it," Long Ball said as if reminiscing about his childhood while showing me the cottage.

Long Ball opened the back door of the cottage, which led out to the beach. There was a porch with a swing and two well-weathered rocking chairs. Even though we were tired, we just sat in the rocking chairs listening to the waves roll up onto the shore. We talked some more about Long Ball's family's summer vacations before we went to bed.

That morning, we went to the Glen Eden Country Club, ate breakfast, and played a round of golf. Long Ball came in at two under par for a sixty-eight. I shot a respectable seventy-six.

For some reason that night, I could not sleep very well. I felt as if I was on guard duty. I had a flashback when I was in Afghanistan after serving in Iraq. Our outpost was on top of a hill, which allowed us to give artillery support to our troops in the valley. I was still fresh. I was in there less than thirty days and had not seen any real action yet, not like Iraq. One night all hell broke loose. I was on guard duty, and I had a feeling we were going to be attacked. And, sure enough, we were. I heard mortar rounds coming in on top of us just as someone else shouted, "Incoming!"

The sky lit up to reveal hundreds of Taliban attacking us. The fighting was fierce. The Taliban were overrunning us. I went through so much ammo, and they just kept on coming. I didn't have time to think about killing someone or whom I was killing. All the training we had was automatic. However, I do remember killing this one guy. He came up over the sandbags and his gun jammed. I would have been a goner. He had me dead on. But my gun jammed as well. I grabbed my KA-Bar knife just as he lunged at me trying to hit me with the butt of his AK-47. I moved just before he landed on top of me and slashed his right leg. He freaked out and came towards me again. This time I stabbed him in his right shoulder with my KA-Bar still in him. I grabbed him and did a circle throw flipping him over me. He was stunned and groggy from the throw. I removed my KA-Bar from his shoulder. With both hands, I plunged my KA-Bar into his chest. He made a weak attempt at grabbing my hands as I took one finishing thrust of my KA-Bar driving it deeper inside him, killing him. What took seconds seemed like an hour of fighting.

The last thing I remember was the Apache Helicopters firing rockets on top of them. They were so close to us I could see the pilots waving at us and giving us the thumbs up as they passed by. The CO must have radioed that we were being overrun and had no choice but to have the A10s come in with their GAU-8 Gatling Guns to clean things up.

As the sun was coming up, I came to. I looked around and saw the devastation firsthand what these Warthogs can do. The entire outpost had bodies of dead Taliban scattered across the north side of our compound where they launched their main offensive. From what I heard later that morning we had a high body count. One hundred and eighty-two Taliban killed. We lost eight guys that night. I struggled to get up. I found another gun and picked it up. Out of the corner of my eye, I saw movement. A wounded Taliban reached for his AK-47. That's about as far as he got before I gave him his last rites.

I must have sat by that window for several hours looking for something to happen before I fell asleep. Before I knew it, Long Ball was knocking at the door.

"Time to get up Clancy," Long Ball said opening my door and finding me still asleep in the chair. He came over and shook me out of my slumber.

"Come on buddy wake up," he said shaking me with his left hand.

I jumped up and tackled Long Ball to the ground before I realized where I was.

"Clancy! Clancy! It's me Long Ball!" he shouted trying to get my attention.

234

"Oh my god, are you okay?" I asked, knowing that I could have killed him.

"Yeah, I'm fine," Long Ball said.

"I'm sorry Long Ball, I had a flashback," I said. "I couldn't sleep last night so I sat up looking out the window. It reminded me of when I was in Afghanistan pulling guard duty."

"Well, you acted like you were still there and you were about to kill me. Did you see anything out there Clancy?" Long Ball asked.

"Just a couple of cats. Call it what you will. It just felt like something was going on. If anything happened, I didn't see it," I said trying to sound reassuring.

"Well, that's comforting to know," Long Ball said.

I took a nice long hot shower, got dressed, and came out to the front room placing my bags by the front door. Long Ball was packed and ready to go. I could smell freshly brewed coffee that Long Ball must have made. I went over to the kitchenette and opened the cupboard where the coffee mugs were. I took one of the mugs and filled it up. Inside one of the drawers, I found some packets of cream and sugar and poured them in.

Long Ball was sitting on the back porch drinking from his mug. I went outside and pulled up a chair to sit with him at the table. It was a cool misty morning with the marine layer rolling in from the ocean. You could see the sun trying to break through and burn away the marine layer.

"You know Clancy, I love the sound of the waves coming in. It's very relaxing. You know what I mean?"

"I sure do," I said. "What's wrong? You look like you're a million miles away."

"I'm just reminiscing how innocent it was when I was a little kid and didn't have to worry about anything. My dad took care of us. He used to take me and my brother out to a special spot and fish when we came here. We had so much fun together. It seemed like he wanted to show us things to help make us become men. I really admired my dad. Our vacations were something we looked forward to every year. You hear so many terrible things about Black families and fathers not being there. My dad was one of the fathers who was there for his wife and kids. He never beat my mother. If they were arguing, they never argued in front of us. My dad always showered us with love. He always hugged and kissed my mom."

"It sounds like you had some precious moments with him and this place," I said looking at my watch.

"We should probably get going, eh Clancy?" Long Ball asked, getting up from his chair and sipping the last few drops of coffee from his mug.

I followed Long Ball inside and took one final look around the room to make sure we didn't forget anything.

We stepped outside with our bags in hand and Long Ball quickly put them down.

"Since it is an unusually cool morning, I'm going to warm up the Maserati before we get in," Long Ball said.

I looked over at Long Ball just as he pushed the remote starter button on the key fob. Neither one of us expected what happened next. The explosion knocked both of us back onto the front porch of the cottage slamming me into the door and Long Ball into the side of the building. Several large shards of glass from the front windows narrowly missed Long Ball's right arm by a few inches.

Flames and smoke from the explosion shot up into the air. Pieces of the car were still falling back onto the ground.

I looked over at Long Ball as he brushed debris off his face and clothes.

"What the hell was that?" I asked, trying to get up. I felt something warm oozing from the back of my head. Reaching around with my left hand I felt the wet spot and looked at the blood on my hand. I managed to get up and make it down the steps. Both of us staggered over to the crumpled metal that once was his pride and joy.

"My beautiful car! My beautiful car!" Long Ball shouted in disbelief.

"Hey! There's someone over here! Corpsman!" I shouted ignoring my own pain to help this man lying on the ground. But this wasn't some stranger. I couldn't believe it. The man lying next to the remains of the car was Leonard Ellis.

"Leonard, what are you doing here? Don't tell me you tried to kill us. Why?" I asked, still in shock from the blast. I took off my belt and used it as a tourniquet for the stump that once was Leonard's right arm.

"I haven't seen wounds like this since Afghanistan," I said looking at Long Ball as other people came over to help.

"An ambulance is on its way," this guy said as he hung up from his cell phone and attached it to the clip on his belt.

More and more people came out of their cottages to see what all the commotion was about. Luckily, no one else was hurt from what I could tell. I heard the sirens getting closer as Leonard reached for my shirt with his good hand pulling me closer to him and saying, "19th Hole!" It was the last thing he said as he took his final breath.

For a small town, it didn't take very long for the police to get here. A helicopter landed across the street at the shopping mall with three men and a woman climbing out. Two of the men wore windbreakers with ATF written on the back of their jackets. The other man and woman wore similar jackets except the FBI was printed on the back. Once the authorities realized that Leonard was dead and wasn't going anywhere, they just covered his body with a blue tarp.

The police cordoned off the area with yellow crime scene tape to keep the onlookers back. Pieces of debris were scattered 100 feet across the entire parking lot in every direction. To be on the safe side the police brought in bomb-sniffing dogs with them to inspect the rest of the parking lot to see if there were any other bombs around. Leonard's body lay still as all three agencies worked around him as they made their investigations into what happened.

"Clancy, what was Leonard trying to tell you before he died?" asked Long Ball.

"You wouldn't believe it. He referred to the 19th Hole. I didn't tell you about this Long Ball. When they found Jorge Rodriguez's body at Wild Creek, there was a matchbook on top of his desk with a 19th Hole logo on it."

"What are you going to do Clancy?"

"I got no choice; I got to call Tanya and tell her about the explosion. This could be the break we are looking for," I said dialing Tanya's number on my cell phone. "There's no answer, it's going into her voicemail," I said hanging up.

"Clancy, you better leave her a message anyway," Long Ball suggested.

"Yeah, I suppose you're right," I said pushing the redial button. Again, it went to voicemail, this time I left a message.

"Tanya, it's me, Clancy. Remember Leonard Ellis, the guy I told you about at the funeral talking with the O'Brien's?" He was a member of Pinewood. Earlier this morning he died trying to kill us. He planted a bomb on Long Ball's Maserati. Fortunately, Long Ball used his remote starter to start the car. The bomb exploded while Leonard was in the process of planting the device when it went off. However, he was able to utter something to me before he died, he said 19th Hole," I said.

"Tanya, can you help me and check on the 19th Hole? See if it is a restaurant, golf shop, or something for me. Also, I need you to do a background check on Leonard Ellis too?"

"Do you think Tanya will help you, Clancy?" Long Ball asked.

"I hope so," I said turning towards Long Ball. "There goes another good day of golf. How come every time I play well, someone gets killed?"

"Well Clancy, I suggest you start having a few bad rounds; especially when you play with me," Long Ball said as we both watched Wade Miller drive up, looking at all the commotion.

The paramedics left us after attending to our wounds.

"What's all this?" asked Wade, getting out of his car, and coming over to us.

It's what's left of my new Maserati," Long Ball said as he looked at the pieces of his beautiful car.

"Thanks for coming Wade," I said shaking his hand.

"What are you doing here Wade?" Long Ball asked.

"I asked him to come up Long Ball. I'm glad I called you last night and asked you to drive up here," I said.

"Did anyone get hurt?" Wade asked.

"Only Leonard," I said.

"What?"

"See that blue tarp over there? That's Leonard's body," Long Ball said pointing in that direction.

"Why?" Wade asked.

"We don't know. The only thing that Leonard was able to say was the 19th Hole," I said.

"He was still alive when you got to him?" Wade asked.

"His arm was blown off. I told Long Ball that I haven't seen anything like that since I was in Afghanistan."

"What do you make of this, Clancy?" Wade asked.

"The tie-in has to be with the 19th Hole. But I don't understand why Leonard would turn on us and try to kill us. We didn't do anything to aggravate him and make him want to kill us, did we?" I asked.

"It's got to be deeper than that Clancy," Wade said.

"Is it okay if we put our bags in your car?" I asked.

"Sure, no problem," Wade said.

Long Ball comes out of the cottage carrying his golf clubs and says, "I'm glad you talked me into taking my clubs inside last night Clancy."

"Me too, Long Ball, me too," I said going back into the cottage to get my bag and golf clubs.

We were just about finishing loading all the bags and golf clubs into Wade's car when one of the men from the helicopter approached us.

"I'm Inspector Lee Nelson with the FBI," he said as he introduced himself, but not shaking hands with any of us. "Can you tell me what you all are doing here?" he asked.

I decided to be quiet at first and let Long Ball do the talking.

"I'm Al 'Long Ball' Jackson, we're on our way to Spokane, Washington. I'm playing in the U.S. Senior Open which starts in the next few days."

"You're not the Long Ball Jackson, are you?" Inspector Nelson asked.

"Yes, I am," Long Ball replied.

242

"I've watched you play. My thirteen-year-old thinks you're the greatest. What's the story on these two?" He asked pointing to me and Wade.

"I know you are aware of the murders of the Black golfers recently," Long Ball said.

"Yes sir, I am. It's a real tragedy. I can assure you that the FBI is doing all they can to solve these murders," the Inspector said.

"I just buried my niece, Nina Jackson, a few days ago. Nina played at Stanford. Harry Clancy and Wade Miller came down for the funeral. And Harry here is a private investigator that I hired to protect me," Long Ball said putting his hand on my shoulder.

"Well Clancy, it looks like you almost botched this one up and got yourself and your client killed if you ask me," Inspector Nelson said.

I didn't like the FBI to begin with, and I definitely do not like this guy. First off, I don't know you and you certainly do not call me Clancy. Only my friends and people I like get that privilege. "You bet, I guess you're right on that one, eh Nelson?"

"Please don't tell me we're going to have an attitude problem are we now boys?" the Inspector asked.

"No sir, everything is fine sir," Wade said.

"Who are you?"

"I'm Wade Miller. I work with Mr. Clancy."

"Doing what?"

"I chase things down for him," Wade explained.

"That sounds exciting," Inspector Nelson said. "What about the dead guy, Leonard Ellis? Do you all know him?"

"Yes, we do. Leonard was a member of Pinewood Golf Association, as we are as well. Nina was in the junior golf program that Pinewood put together. However, it was interesting that Leonard attended her funeral," I said.

"How's that?" Inspector Nelson asked.

"Leonard has only been with the group for just about a year. He never really knew Nina. So, we were really surprised to see Leonard here for the funeral.

"Do you have any idea why he would want to kill you, Mr. Jackson?"

"Not really, I don't understand it at all. I've never done anything to him, nor have I met him," Long Ball explained.

"What about you Clancy and you Mr. Miller? You two have any gripes with him?" Inspector Nelson asked.

Wade and I both looked at each other shaking our heads not at all. Knowing full well that neither of us could stand Leonard. We were both relieved to see that he died so we didn't have to do it ourselves. Also, we would not be going to jail because of it.

"Poor Leonard didn't know what a blessing it was for him to blow himself up," Long Ball said.

"What do you mean by that?" Inspector Nelson asked.

"From what I was told, not a lot of people liked him," Long Ball said.

"Leonard was a jerk from the first time he joined Pinewood. I wanted to punch him several times and I know Wade did too," I said. "Isn't that right Wade?"

"Yeah, that's true," Wade answered reluctantly.

"You still haven't answered my question. What are you doing here?" the Inspector asked again.

"Well, you see Inspector Nelson, I hate to fly. Clancy and I decided to take our time and drive up to Spokane. We wanted to get a few rounds of golf in along the way. This was our first stop. We played yesterday and we were thinking of maybe playing another round today. Now with all this mess, I don't think that playing today would be in the realm of possibilities," Long Ball said.

"You have a point," the Inspector said.

"Inspector, can I ask you a question?" I asked.

"Sure."

"Are you making any headway on the Joey Conrad case? We were planning to stop in Corvallis and talk with the authorities there," I said.

"All I can tell you is that the investigation is ongoing, and we have nothing conclusive yet," the Inspector told us as an officer approached us.

"Hello gentlemen, I'm Officer David Margo and my boss told me to get your identification. Would you please give me your driver's license?" Officer Margo asked.

All three of us took our licenses out of our wallets and handed them to the officer.

"Thank you, gentlemen, I'll be right back."

Officer Margo went back to his superior and showed him our identification. I could tell that his boss told him to run a background check on us because Officer Margo climbed into his police car and radioed in our information. We weren't paying any attention to him.

Inspector Nelson asked, "Could I get your autograph for my son?" Long Ball gladly gave it to him.

But as soon as he was done signing the page on Inspector Nelson's notepad Officer Margo came back over to us with his gun drawn and shouted, "Mr. Clancy, you are under arrest for the murder of Patty Hill!"

Inspector Nelson and the rest of the law enforcement people all had their guns drawn on

246

me. Officer Margo slammed me to the ground and cuffed me.

"What's this all about?" I asked as Officer Margo and another police officer picked me up off the ground.

"Patty Hill was found murdered in her office last night by the janitor," Officer Margo explained.

"I didn't kill her," I pleaded. "She was alive when I left her," I said.

That didn't stop them as they escorted me into a squad car. Once inside, I watched the officers talk to Wade and Long Ball. Wade and Long Ball must have checked out okay because they were handed back their identification and were free to go.

CHAPTER THIRTEEN

AM I DREAMING?

It was several hours before they got me processed at the local jail. Officer Margo did say that they were going to extradite me to Palo Alto and fly me back down to face charges of first-degree murder. I had to ask myself, what did I do to deserve this? Someone is setting me up for a terrible fall, but why me? I guess the sooner I get on that plane, the sooner I can get this whole situation cleaned up.

Upon my arrival, Joe Bowman and Tanya Jones were there to greet me at the airport. Detective Bowman took delight in shoving me into the police van, which caused me to hit my head on the floor. With the handcuffs on, I couldn't brace myself for the fall. I wanted to spit in his face as he helped me up off the floor of the van, but I briefly got a bit of wisdom and decided I better not. The look of disgust on Tanya's face said it all.

"Clancy, I don't know what to think of you! I can't understand how you could have killed

Patty Hill," Tanya said with a tone in her voice that I had never heard before.

"What evidence do they have that I killed her?" I asked Tanya.

"They have the murder weapon, your sand wedge," she said. "Your prints are on it, Clancy."

"Of course, they are, it's my club. Can't you see this is a setup?" I asked as we arrived back at the Palo Alto Police Station.

Long lines of reporters and cameras from the local TV stations were at the back entrance waiting to get a glimpse of me. Everyone was shouting questions at me wanting to know why I killed Coach Hill, even Julie Monroe, "Mr. Clancy, why did you kill Patty Hill?" Ms. Monroe also asked the detectives, "What evidence do you have on Mr. Clancy?" Tanya and Detective Bowman did not say a word. All the reporters were trying to get the scoop on what was happening as we walked up the ramp to go inside.

"Who would want to frame me?" I asked Tanya.

"I don't know Clancy. Patty was bludgeoned to death with your club. It was a brutal murder scene, Clancy," Tanya said.

"Too bad California doesn't use the gas chamber anymore. I would love to see you squirm when they drop the cyanide pellets. Lethal Injection is way too easy for you buddy boy. You deserve to suffer how Patty Hill suffered," Joe Bowman said.

"Knock it off, Joe!" Tanya yelled back at Detective Bowman.

Tanya and Detective Bowman made it to the door that led me inside to be booked, fingerprinted, and photographed. I was relieved to be away from the mob outside. However, this is the last place I expected to be. I have never been to jail before as a criminal. This is a very demoralizing experience for me. They strip searched me as well as probed me for contraband to make sure I wasn't smuggling anything inside.

There were six of us that were being processed at the same time. I was fingerprinted, photographed, and searched. A correctional officer made me sign my name on top of a large manila envelope. All my personal belongings, like my watch, keys, wallet, and whatever change I had on me were inside. Signing my name at this check-in counter did not make me feel like I was checking in at the Holiday Inn.

"Don't worry gentlemen you'll receive your property back at the time of your release. For some of you, your clothes will be out of style by the time you get out," a correctional officer said smiling.

I know exactly what he means. Many of these guys won't be coming out soon. Before I left, Long Ball told me not to worry he was going to call his attorney and have him come see me tomorrow morning.

On a bench against the wall were piles of white underwear that the jailer gave us. Wearing only our underwear and white crew socks he led us down a light green corridor and told us not to walk outside the yellow line on the floor. The jailer led us to another area with a heavily meshed screen window. There was another jailer behind the window who gave each of us a pair of standard orange jail uniforms for us to wear. And don't forget the matching jailhouse slippers.

"All right gentlemen after you have received your uniforms follow the yellow line to the next bench. Put your uniforms down on the bench and remain standing until I tell you what to do next," the jailer said.

Unfortunately, this one Black guy did not get the memo and sat down. The jailer came over to him and proceeded to take out his baton and shoved it into his ribs. "Now get your Black butt up boy before I crack this baton over your head. Did I tell you to sit down?" he asked.

"No sir," the Black guy said holding his side as he got back up off the bench.

The rest of us made it over to the bench and stood waiting for our next set of orders. "Gentlemen please proceed to put on your clothing and remain standing until I tell you to move," the jailer said. The Black guy was obedient and none of us said a word. "Okay gents, follow the yellow line to the next window. There you will be issued your bedding," he said.

There is a long counter with several guys behind it. The guy at the window gave us a green blanket, a white sheet, and a pillow. "Keep moving gentlemen. After you get your bedding, hold it in front of you," our jailer said. The guy behind the counter placed a roll of toilet paper on top of our blankets. He also put a baggie on top of the blanket as well, which had a bar of soap, a comb, toothpaste, and a toothbrush.

"Gentlemen, follow me," our jailer said.

Another jailer lined up behind us as they both led us down the corridor to a door that led into the jailhouse. Our jailer spoke into the intercom and the door was unlocked. Our jailer opened it. To my surprise, a set of steel bars faced us. The gate slid open, and we were led inside. The first thing I noticed was the strong smell of urine, sweat, and feces. But what was more noticeable was the noise. Everyone was yelling at us as we walked by. I heard one guy say, "Fresh meat." The faces on these guys looked like they were from the movie Shawshank Redemption.

Look straight ahead gentlemen; no talking allowed," he said as we walked single file through the cellblock.

Again, we stopped in front of another door. This time the jailer took out a key and unlocked the door. Just inside was an intercom and another set of steel bars.

"Charlie, it's me Officer Gordon with six prisoners being escorted to E Block," he said.

At the sound of the buzzer, the steel-barred gate slid open. This area was completely different. It was brand new. It was an open area with round picnic tables that were bolted to the floor. Three benches surrounded each table and were also bolted down to the floor. A total of six people could sit at each table.

A guard came up to us to relieve Officer Gordon. "Thank you, Officer Gordon," the guard said. "Gentlemen you have just entered the modern era of the penal system. We feel that this is the most humane way of treating prisoners."

"Yeah right," an inmate said just loud enough for all of us to hear as he mopped the floor.

"Did you have something to say, Mason?" One of the guards asked as he whacked the inmate with his baton who fell to the floor.

"No sir," Mason groaned as he tried to pull himself off the floor. I started to help him up, but he motioned me with his hand not to help him. I mouthed the words, "thank you," to him as we moved up the stairs to our respective cells. Mason went back to mopping the floor and watched us the whole time. He smiled at me when the guard stopped by my cell. Mason pointed to his chest to let me know that I was

253

going to be with him. I don't know if I should be relieved or if I'm going to be in trouble. I tried to settle into my new digs. I didn't know what to expect. I saw that the bottom bunk was made and that the top bunk was bare. I took the liberty to make my bed and climbed in so I could get some sleep.

Since the six of us were finally settled into our cells the guards turned out the lights. There was a faint glow from the doghouse. I could hear two sets of footsteps approaching my cell and the chatter from a walkie-talkie. Mason entered my cell while the guard waited outside and closed the door giving the final count to the person on the other end of the walkie-talkie. The sound of the door closing and the ensuing locking of it sounded ominous.

"I'm Drew Mason, nice to meet you," as he extended his hand to shake mine.

"I'm Harry Clancy, how are you doing?" I asked.

"All right I guess and you?" he said smiling at me.

Drew looked like he was born to be in jail. He was Black, had a gold front tooth, tattoos on both of his biceps, a shaved head, and was built like Mr. Universe. My guess is he was about 6'5" and weighed in at 255 pounds of pure muscle.

"You're trying to figure out what this place is all about aren't you?" he asked.

"Yeah, I suppose you're right about that," I said.

"Here's what you're looking at from the doghouse. The guards can see the cells in a 360-degree radius. The doghouse extends up six floors in the middle of the cell block. There are three levels of doghouses where the guards can monitor two floors of each cell block. The guards have complete control of everything inside," Drew said.

"That makes sense, doesn't it? After all, we are in jail, aren't we?" I asked.

"What are you in for?" Drew asked.

"First-degree murder," I said to him. "But I didn't do it. I'm innocent," I said.

"You know Harry, we're all innocent, aren't we?" Mason asked.

"No, you don't understand; I really am innocent! I'm a private investigator. It's all a setup," I tried to explain to him.

I told him all about the murders of the Black golfers and the explosion with Leonard. I don't know why, but I feel like I can tell him everything about me. I even told him about Tanya. Here I am telling this guy my complete life story. Why would I do something like that, I asked myself?

"Drew, I don't know why I am opening myself to you like this. It doesn't make any sense," I said.

255

"On the contrary, Harry, it makes perfect sense. God has placed me here at this very moment to help lead you through this ordeal so that His glory can shine forth," Drew said.

Hey, it's bad enough to be locked up, but to be locked up with a Jesus freak is even worse, I said to myself, still trying to size him up.

"Look, I'm not into this God thing. It just doesn't work for me. I'm glad it's helping you. But it's not for me. I had my share of God when I was in grade school and high school. I was raised Catholic. I went to a Catholic grade school and an all-boy Catholic high school. If anything, it caused me to rebel against God," I said.

"Hey, I understand. I'm not trying to force anything on you at all. I just know that God has set me free. I got saved on the inside. I was tore up from the floor up on the outside. I did drugs, alcohol; robbed people, and I was a pimp. I did it all. But one day, I was out on the street with no place to go. I went to a shelter to get some food. There was this one guy that I knew a long time ago, back in the day. He was a hustler who had a lot of money and women. One day, he got busted and lost everything."

I sat there listening to his story.

"He asked me to go to the liquor store with him. I stayed in the car while he went inside. The next thing I know, I hear shots. He comes running out of the store over to the car. The store owner comes out bleeding. He's able to fire off a

256

shot which kills my friend. The store owner collapses in front of the car and dies from his wounds."

"My god, you're kidding me?" I asked, still mesmerized by his story.

"Now, I ended up getting arrested and charged with murder as an accomplice, doing life."

"Mason, if I can do anything to help you when I get out, I will."

"Thanks, I appreciate that, Harry."

The next day, Long Ball's attorney, Marcus Morrison, meets with me in the Palo Alto County Jail visiting room and goes over the charges of first-degree murder.

"Mr. Morrison, I am innocent! All I wanted to do was meet with Patty Hill to discuss Nina Jackson's and Sarah O'Brien's relationship on the golf team," I pleaded.

"Mr. Clancy, you were the last one to see her alive, according to her secretary. Mrs. Hill did not have any other visitors that day. Mrs. Hill was found bludgeoned to death on the floor of her office after you left with your bloody sand wedge lying next to her," he explained.

"Listen Mr. Morrison, I'm telling you the truth. Long Ball and I played golf at Pebble Beach the other day. Someone must have stolen my sand wedge. I'm sure of it."

"Were your golf clubs in your possession the whole time?" he asked.

257

"Yes, I believe so."

"Not a good answer, Mr. Clancy."

I sat there trying to remember what happened after we played. Then it dawned on me. Our caddies cleaned our clubs for us.

"Wait a minute. The only time I didn't have the clubs was when our caddies took them from us to clean them after our round," I said. Long Ball and I played at Glen Eden Country Club yesterday, but I did not use my sand wedge at all during the round," I said.

Later that morning, I was seated at the defense table with Mr. Morrison at the Palo Alto Superior Court for my arraignment.

"What's your plea, Mr. Clancy?" the judge asked.

Both Mr. Morrison and I stand up to give my response.

"Not guilty, your honor," I said.

The victim's family is outraged. Patty Hill's father, Mike Davis, stands up and starts yelling. "You'll pay, you bloody son of a bitch, if it's the last thing I do!"

"Bail is set at one million dollars," the judge says. The judge bangs the gavel one final time and gets up to leave the courtroom.

I turn around and wave at Tanya, Long Ball, and Wade as the bailiff takes me back to my jail cell.

The next morning, Wade came to visit me at the Palo Alto County Jail visiting room. Wade looks at me as I walk in, wearing an orange jail outfit. I sat down at one of the six plexiglass booths facing the visitors. I picked up the phone and was excited to see Wade.

"Hey, Clancy, how are you holding up?"

"I'm okay. I tell you, it's a trip being locked up in here."

"Clancy, I spoke to Leonard's cousin Jamie Ellis and told him what happened. Apparently, Leonard mailed a package to Jamie a couple of days before he died with a sealed envelope inside. The instructions said to be opened upon Leonard's untimely death."

"Do you think being blown to bits is untimely, Wade?"

We both laugh.

"I believe so."

"Wade, this is great news. I can only hope the package has enough information to clear my name. Wade, I need you to go get that package. I've got to get out of here! Will you do that for me?"

"Sure, no problem. I've already discussed it with Jamie. He said that he would wait for me before he opens it."

"How's Long Ball holding up?" I asked.

"He's not too happy about flying up to Spokane. He always gets airsick. The Pro-Am starts tomorrow, and he needs to be there. Also, I told him about the letter. I convinced him that we have to fly up there and do this for Clancy."

"Thanks, Wade."

Wade has two airline tickets for him and Long Ball.

"We fly out today at 11:10."

"That's great, Wade. You're all packed and ready to go.?"

'Yes, I just got to stop by and get Long Ball. Look, Clancy, hang in there. We'll get you out."

The guard came over and tapped me on my shoulder, letting me know that my time was up.

"I'll see you around, Wade; thanks for all of your help," I said, hanging up the phone.

Wade stood there, watching me leave to return to my cell. I turned around and waved one last time.

"I'm amazed at all the different types of people that are locked up inside this place. I passed the television area and heard that they were watching The Price Is Right. Some of the guys were yelling at the contestants saying the price is lower. When I got back to my cell, it was empty. Mason was gone. His bunk was made. I decided to lie down and try to get some sleep. I must have been in a deep sleep because 45 minutes later when the buzzer sounded for lunch, it startled me. I was totally disoriented. Standing by me was Mason.

"Hey Harry, get up! We got five minutes to get in line before we go eat."

The correctional officers were doing the second head count for the day. All prisoners had to stand outside of their cells and wait to be counted. This is one time when you can look around and see everyone. Once everyone was accounted for, they led us to the cafeteria. A steady line of inmates waited for their food. From the looks of it, bologna sandwiches, applesauce, an orange, and milk were the main menu items for the day. One thing for sure, the correctional officers ran a tight ship. They expect everything to be in order.

After lunch, we went outside to the yard for an hour. You could see the Hispanics, Blacks, whites, and even the Asians staying together within their own group. I tried to stay off by myself and walk around the track, but this one brother came over to me. However, he backed off when he saw Mason coming over to me.

"You need to watch him, Clancy. He's a sweet guy," Mason said.

"So."

"You don't get it, do you? He was going to make a play on you," explained Mason.

"Oh, hell no!"

"Watch out. He's got some friends, and they will try to get you by yourself," warned Mason.

The rest of the day was uneventful. I laid around in my bunk and tried to read the Bible, but that put me to sleep. That is exactly what I needed. The guards did another count before dinner and another final count for the evening at lights out.

Chapter Fourteen

The Good News

The next day, at 5:30, they woke us up for breakfast, and the whole cycle began all over again.

But one thing happened that I didn't expect. A guard came over to my cell and told me I had a visitor. To my surprise, it was Wade. "What the hell are you doing here?" I asked.

"Clancy, I got some great news. You should be able to get out of her today."

"How?"

"Well, you know how Long Ball is with airplanes?"

"Did he get sick?"

'Yes, he did. I gave him an airsick bag just in time for him to hurl," Wade said, laughing.

I was smiling, too. I have flown with Long Ball enough times to watch him get sick on a plane.

"After we landed, we met with Phil Roberts outside baggage claim. He said he heard what

263

happened to you on the news. It's the biggest story in town."

"What else did he say?" I asked.

"Phil said he heard about Leonard and that he got the information you wanted to check on."

"Really, that's great. What is it?" I asked.

"Well, Clancy, it turns out that Leonard owed some people a lot of money."

"How much are we talking about?"

"You're not going to believe this, Clancy."

"Try me."

"About $300,000. I guess Leonard likes to gamble. Oops, he liked to gamble," Wade said with a smirk on his face.

"Any idea who he owed the money to?

"Yeah, Phil said, it was some guy named Garcia."

"Wow!"

"Phil dropped us off at Jamie's house so we could check out what was inside the package."

"Tell me."

"Clancy, Jamie opened the envelope and read the letter. He played the tape that will completely exonerate you from these charges."

"You're kidding?"

"No, I'm not. I'm serious."

"What does it say?"

"Clancy, we all sat around and listened to the tape first, then read the letter. Everything on that tape is in the letter. We were really shocked by what it said. Look, Clancy, I made a copy of the letter and brought it with me. Let me read it to you."

"It starts with Leonard saying:"

'Hi Jamie, if you are listening to this tape, it means I am dead. It's not much of a surprise to you, I guess. You always told me that I'm not going to live long if I continue to live this way. Well, you were right, as usual. I got into some big trouble and owed some people a lot of money. You know how I always liked to go to Las Vegas and gamble? I borrowed some money and lost it all, about $300,000. I had to skip town and try to make a clean break. Unfortunately, they caught up with me. They were ready to kill me; however, they said that there was a way for me to get out of it. They wanted me to do a hit for them. They had a contract out on some Black golfer at Oregon State. Some guy named Joey Conrad. It didn't make sense, but I had to do it. It was either him or me. I killed the others, too, except for Nina. This guy named Garcia killed her. He gave me a list of people he wanted killed. He also told me that he was going to frame Clancy. Somehow, Garcia got Clancy's golf club to set him up. My next target was going to be Long Ball. Watch out for the 19th Hole. Goodbye, Jamie."

Wade folded up the letter and put it back into his pocket.

"Clancy, everyone had that same shocked look on their faces, just like you, when they heard

265

the tape. But it is a relief for us to know the answers. Even though Jamie was upset about his cousin, everyone was excited that we could get you off the hook. I told everyone we need to go straight to the police."

"What happened?" I asked.

"You should have seen us. Long Ball, Jamie, and I go running into the entrance of the Spokane Police Department and come face-to-face with the desk sergeant. We're all excited to tell him we want to see the police chief, Mark Larson. I told him we have information on who murdered the Black golfers."

"I can only imagine what Chief Larson had to say," I said.

"The desk sergeant calls his superior to get approval. Another officer comes out to meet everyone and leads us into Chief Larson's office. Chief Larson comes in and seems interested in our additional information about the unsolved murders. We showed him the letter and played the tape. What do you think? It clearly shows that Clancy has been framed, doesn't it?"

"What was his reaction?"

"You're not going to believe it. He says Leonard's confession works for me, but it is speculative about Clancy. Everything is straightforward with Patty Hill. I don't see how they can let him go."

"Wade, did you really expect to get any support from him?"

"Clancy, I had to go straight off on him. Long Ball had to restrain me. Chief, you need to call the Palo Alto, P.D. and talk to them! You don't want to help Clancy! You still hold him responsible for your son's death on that drug bust that went bad! You ruined his life! He was a good cop!"

"Wade, I always knew if I ever had anything to do with the Spokane Police Department, Chief Larson would be a stumbling block."

"Well, Clancy, Chief Larson yelled for us to get the hell out of his office. However, he wanted us to leave the letter and the tape with him."

"What did you tell him?"

"I told him, hell no!"

"He must have blown a gasket."

"He sure did. He told me if I don't leave it with him, he'll have me arrested for withholding evidence."

"So, what did you do?"

"I reluctantly left him the tape and the letter."

"Did you give him the original?" I asked.

"No way, Clancy. I made several copies."

"That's good. I need to get a copy to my attorney."

"I already did that, Clancy. I called Marcus Morrison yesterday afternoon and told him what happened. I told him that Chief Larson was being very uncooperative. I also told him I had to hand over the tape and letter to the Chief."

"What did Morrison say?"

"He said that he was concerned about the tape being in Chief Larson's possession. I told him not to worry because I gave him copies. I have the originals. Mr. Morrison said he wanted me to email him a copy of the letter so he could try to get you out of jail. But he said that he really needed to get the tape. He wanted to know if I could send it to him overnight. I told him to be on the safe side, that I could fly it down myself. He said that's great. I told him I could be back down there by ten this evening. I also told him to meet me at the Santa Clara County Airport.

"What did he say?"

"He said that's great and that he'll be there."

"How did you get down so quick?" I asked.

"I flew my Diamond DA42. After I got through with Mr. Morrison, I called the flight office at Felts Field and asked them to have my plane fueled and ready to go in the next thirty minutes. Jamie and Long Ball dropped me off at the airport. After I did my walkaround and pre-flight check, I took off and met Mr. Morrison."

"What time did you get in?"

"Right at ten o'clock, like I said."

"Was Mr. Morrison there?"

"Yes, he was waiting for me next to his Mercedes. I gave him the tape and letter.

Mr. Morrison wanted me to get in the car with him and listen to the tape. It was on one of those micro cassette tapes.

He had a microcassette player with him.

"What did he say after he heard it?"

"Clancy, he said that he didn't see a problem with you getting released."

"That's great, Wade. Thank you so much for all of your help."

"No problem, Clancy. That's why I'm here to tell you the good news. This morning, there was a press conference on the steps of the Santa Clara County Jail. Mr. Morrison spoke with Police Chief Gordon Beals of the Palo Alto Police Department and presented this new evidence to him. Chief Beals said he had an announcement concerning the murders of Jorge Rodriguez and Patty Hill. The press was there Chief Beals said that the murders of Jorge Rodriguez and Patty may be linked to the murders of Nina Jackson and the other Black golfers who were also killed. He said earlier this morning that he had spoken with Police Chief Mark Larson of the Spokane Police Department. Chief Beals said that Chief Larson has enough evidence to implicate Leonard Ellis as the person responsible for these murders over the past several months."

I was elated to hear the news. But I was surprised to hear what Wade said next.

"Clancy, there were cameras flashing, reporters jockeying for a better position, and shouting questions. But we were stunned that Chief Beals didn't say a word about you, Clancy. Fortunately, one of the reporters from Action 2 News addressed that issue to Chief Beals. Julie Monroe asked if this means that Harry Clancy is innocent of the murder of Patty Hill."

"What did he say about that?"

"Chief Beals said that he couldn't comment on that right now and that Mr. Clancy will remain in our custody until further notice."

"My god, you're kidding me. What more does he want?" I asked.

"Hold on, Clancy, it gets better. Right then, Mr. Morrison yells out that he has the original tape from Leonard Ellis, which will clearly prove that the police have the wrong man in custody. The real killer of Patty Hill and Jorge Rodriguez is Manuel Garcia. A soundman puts a microphone up to the tape player that Mr. Morrison is holding. Everyone is listening to the tape over the loudspeakers, and it clearly exonerates Harry Clancy as the killer."

"Thank God; for Mr. Morrison," I said.

CHAPTER FIFTEEN

THE UNEXPECTED

Later that day, I'm in front of the Santa Clara County Jail main gate as a free man. Guess who is out front waiting for me? Tanya. I couldn't believe it. She comes up to me and gives me a hug.

"Clancy, I knew you were innocent."

"Thank you for having faith in me, Tanya."

"Speaking of faith, what are you doing this evening?"

"I hope to be spending it with you," I said.

"I'd love to have you spend it with me, Harry."

I didn't see Wade waiting for me until Tanya, and I started walking over to her car.

"What about me, Clancy?"

"It's okay, Wade; I'll drop him off at your hotel," Tanya said.

"Okay, you two, have fun. I'll catch you later, Clancy."

Man, I am so excited to be with Tanya. I wonder what she has in store for me as we drive off. To my dismay, Tanya pulls into the parking lot of New Hope Christian Center.

"What's this all about?" I asked.

"You said you wanted to spend the evening with me, didn't you?"

"Yes."

About twenty teenagers come running up to Tanya as we enter the chapel, shouting, "Hello, Sister Tanya!"

"Listen, everyone. We have a special guest with us this evening, Mr. Harry Clancy. So, I want all of you to be on your best behavior," Tanya said.

As soon as Tanya finished talking, all the kids came over to me and shook my hand.

"Okay, everyone, please gather around," motioned Tanya.

I watch as the group forms a circle to join hands.

"Andrew, will you lead us in prayer?" Tanya asked.

I couldn't make out all that Andrew was saying, but it was something like, "Dear Lord bless this rehearsal..."

Afterwards, Tanya had them go up to the choir stand as she directs them through several songs. The music sounds so good that I catch myself stomping my foot to the beat. The group came up to me after rehearsal and thanked me for coming.

Later, in Tanya's car as we were driving to the hotel, Tanya says, "I saw you stomping your feet to the music. I didn't know you liked gospel music."

"They were really good, and I liked it."

"How long have you been doing this Tanya?"

"I've been coming to this church for almost twenty years and directing the choir for the past ten years."

"But, why religion?" I asked.

"Because after what I did to you, I felt I had to get grounded in something."

"Why did you leave me hanging at the altar, Tanya?"

"I know I owe you an explanation, but I can't. Not just yet."

We get to the hotel, and Tanya is about to drop me off. "I guess this is it? Thanks, Tanya. Let me know if anything turns up on Garcia, okay?" I asked.

"I will. Give my best to Wade and Long Ball."

"I will call you after the tournament."

Next thing I know, she's gone. That's it. I thought we would be spending the night together or something.

Chapter Sixteen

Double the Trouble

Wade and I flew back up to Spokane early the next morning, just in time to be on the bag with Long Ball for the fourth and final round of the U.S. Senior Open. Long Ball doesn't tee off until later in the afternoon in the last pairing. Long Ball is tied with Danny Williams for the lead. As I head over to meet Long Ball at the driving range, my cell phone rings. It's Tanya.

"This is Clancy."

"Harry, it's me, Tanya. I'm at the airport on my way up to Spokane. I should be there around 5:30. I have some great news for you," she said.

At that moment, my cell phone signal dropped. "Hello, Tanya? Tanya, can you hear me?" I put the phone back in my pocket, hoping she would call me back. I met Long Ball at the driving range.

"Guess who just called me Long Ball?"

"Tanya," he said, handing me his driver.

"Yeah, she's coming up to Spokane. She'll be here later this afternoon. Tanya told me she has some great news for me."

"Come on, Clancy. I tee off in fifteen minutes. What's the news?"

"I wish I knew. I lost the signal before I had a chance to find out."

"Don't worry, Clancy. You'll find out soon enough. I need you to focus on helping me win this tournament right now."

"You're right. Let's get this done."

Long Ball and Danny Williams are both playing great and are still tied going into the Par 3-17th. As we are walking towards the 17th green, I see a greens keeper coming over towards us. To my shock and horror, I see the man pull a gun out from underneath his coveralls. I pulled out my Beretta to shoot the guy before he could get a shot off. It is complete chaos. Spectators are running, screaming, and diving to the ground to find cover. I rush over to the greenskeeper.

"Long Ball, this must be Manuel Garcia," I said, rolling the man over. Manuel Garcia's wig comes off. A crop of bright red hair crowns the top of his head. I yank at the beard and pull it away, and to my surprise, it is Johnny O'Brien.

"Oh, my god!"

The police and paramedics rushed over to us. The police officers have their guns drawn on me. An officer shouts, "Freeze! Put the gun down and get on the ground! Now!"

I get down on the ground, and the officer comes over to cuff me but is stopped by Chief Larson.

"Stop, help the man up. I saw everything," Chief Larson says.

"Thanks, Chief," I said.

"That was quick thinking, Clancy. Excellent job," he said.

An hour later, after the body was removed and things were cleaned up, play resumed.

Danny Williams and Long Ball are still tied at 7 under, going into the Par-5 18th. Long Ball hits a long drive and decides to lay up on his second shot. Danny Williams tries to reach the green in two and lands in the water. Long Ball gets on the green in three and has a four-footer to win. Danny Williams is on in four and makes par. Long Ball sinks his birdie putt and wins. The crowd is roaring. Both players shake hands.

I walked up to Long Ball. "Fantastic job, Long Ball," I said, giving him a hug. The pressure was off, and the case was over.

"We can finally relax Clancy. Thanks for saving my life," said Long Ball.

After the trophy presentation, we went back to the locker room to get cleaned up for the championship dinner. We were all seated in the Grand Ballroom at the Diamond Back Country Club when a woman came over to the table where Long Ball and I were sitting. I looked over at her. She had the 19th Hole logo on her uniform.

"Mrs. O'Brien, is that you?" I asked.

Long Ball piped up and said, "No, it isn't. That's Mrs. Williams, Danny's wife."

"She's a twin?"

As soon as I asked that question, I flashed back to Leonard's last words: watch out for the 19th Hole. The 19th Hole is the catering company. This is insane. I remember Mrs. O'Brien saying that she has a catering company. Why would they all be behind all of the killings? As I came to this revelation, I glanced over and saw Tanya coming over to our table. At the same time, Mrs. O'Brien comes out, dropping a tray of food she is carrying. She pulls out a gun. Tanya sees Mrs. O'Brien and pushes Long Ball out of the way, and gets hit by a bullet, seriously wounding her. I still have my Berretta with me, and I'm able to shoot and kill Mrs. O'Brien with a clean headshot. By this time, Mrs. Williams tries to shoot me and misses. I popped off another round and hit Mrs. Williams right in the chest.

As she lies on the ground, Mrs. William looks over at Long Ball and shouts, "You destroyed our lives, you black bastard!"

Danny Williams is horrified that his wife is involved. He is crying as he slides down the floor to hold his wife as she dies in his arms.

"Why?" he asks.

Wade shows up with the police.

"Clancy, Sarah O'Brien, and Pete Williams have both been arrested," Wade said.

I look over and see Tanya being wheeled out on a stretcher by the paramedics.

Tanya looks over to me and says, "You have a son."

Tanya passed out before I could say anything to her.

"A son. What do you mean I have a son?" I asked. The paramedics kept me away from her as they put her into the ambulance.

CHAPTER SEVENTEEN

THE DECISION

Later that night, we were in Tanya's hospital room. Tanya survived the surgery and went on to explain what had happened.

"Harry, you have a son, and he is twenty-three. He is going to Stanford studying to be an attorney."

"I'm confused, Tanya. Can I see him?"

"He should be here any moment. He came up here with me. That's what I was trying to tell you over the phone before you dropped off," she said.

I look and see the door open. In walks this young man who looks just like me.

"Harry Clancy Jones, meet your dad," Tanya says as tears begin to stream down her face.

"He looks just like his father," said Long Ball.

Harry and I embrace, and we both begin to cry.

"Why didn't you tell me?" I asked.

279

"Harry, I didn't want to force you into marrying me. You would have thought I trapped you," explains Tanya.

I decided to get down on one knee beside Tanya's bed. I grabbed her hand and asked, "Tanya, will you marry me?"

Tanya is crying uncontrollably and says, "Yes!"

I get off the floor, lean on the bed, and finally kiss Tanya.

"Tanya and Long Ball, there is one other thing I need both of you to do for me. Will you lead me to Christ?"

Tanya's tears are flowing non-stop as they lead me to Jesus Christ, and I accept Him as my Lord and Savior.

***

Two months later, we are at the New Hope Christian Center. It is crowded with friends and family.

The pastor turns to me and says, "You may kiss your bride."

Tanya and I kiss and turn around to face the people in church.

"Ladies and gentlemen, I am pleased to introduce to you Mr. and Mrs. Harry Clancy," the pastor said, raising his hands to the congregation as we jumped the broom.

I look out into the crowd and see Long Ball, Wade, and members from Pinewood. A big smile comes over my face when I see Drew Mason.

THE END